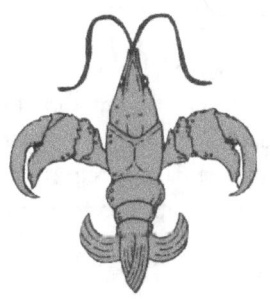

CAJUN

A COLLECTION OF SHORT STORIES

BY PEGGY MARCEAUX

ISBN: 978-1-956581-35-5

Erin Go Bragh Publishing
Canyon Lake, TX

Manufactured in the United States of America
Book Design by Kathleen's Graphics

Table of Contents

BAYOU GAUCHE

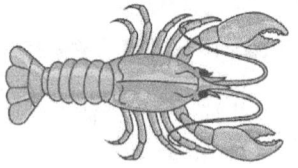

BAYOU GAUCHE

Russell Thibodaux moved his family of seven from Abbeville, Louisiana, in Vermillion Parish, to Bayou Gauche in St. Charles Parish in 1920, it was a rough living, but Russel loved interacting directly with nature. He fished from a pirogue and had his sons trap in the winter while he worked as a carpenter, but the boys had plenty to trap, and he loved working with wood. The first boat that he built was for his family. It was an old shrimper he made from used boards and the nails he could scrounge up from carpentry jobs. Shrimping turned out to be a great addition to the family meals, and feeding his family was foremost on his mind. His wife, Sible took care of sewing the kids' clothes for school and church, while he and his three sons were in charge of putting food on the table. He made his own nets with twine and a shuttle. When he shrimped he discovered he also pulled up nice blue crab. He was elated; that added a luxury to the gumbo pot. Yes, Bayou Gauche was hard on its people, but it beat working in the sugar cane fields in Abbeville and rice prann in Kaplan.

The next fall he completed the houseboat, that is, when he wasn't hired out to do other carpentry work. The houseboat needed to be pretty sizeable, but he wanted out from under Mr. Simoneaux's rent money, as little as it was for a dilapidated old house. That man owned nearly all of Bayou Gauche. Russell wanted to live off the land and pay only for the gas for his pirogue, his houseboat, and whatever the material cost for his wife and children's clothes and shoes. As far as his clothes, he didn't much care. He didn't go to church, and worked all day, so he only needed work clothes. The best thing about it was he owed nothing to the government. The people there paid him in cash for his carpentry skills. Russell had taken his family as completely off the grid as they could be and still be in the middle of people. Sometimes, when he had an excess of shrimp in his net, he sold it to those people, for cash, of course. There was a little bartering, say for canned vegetables, or other staples they didn't have, but that was it.

When Russell finished his house boat, his family moved in. There wasn't much to move since a sewing machine, some material, some primitive table ware, and a cast iron gumbo pot and skillet made up the whole of his family's possessions. The children's school books were on loan from the school, so that was a blessing. Now, Russell's agenda was complete, and there was nothing left to do but, live, fish, trap and make crawfish nets for the best tasting food of the spring. He was happy, but he didn't count on what was coming in the Gulf of Mexico. In 1920, nobody was counting on it. There was no television to tell you there in Bayou Gauche,

One afternoon, he came into the kitchen of the house boat and gently slapped his wife on the rear as she stirred the skillet above the propane stove. "Whutchu got der, Chere? It shore smells good, yeh."

"Mrs. Duhon traded us dis canned okra far some shrimp de udder day, so Ahm makin' sum okra gumbo, and cornbread to go wit it," Sible answered.

"Hot diggy dog," he said and smiled widely.

"And yu, whutchu yu doin, yu?" she asked.

"Ahm about to take de pirogue and see whut's bitin' on de line," he replied.

"Ah hope yu cum back wit sumetin ah can make a cubion wit. Maybe yu can brin' in a redfish, since de wada is churning up so. Nah yu be careful in dat pirogue."

"Ahm dun giv' the boys off to work wit der traps."

"Whut will Mrs Perygene tink? she asked,''

"Ah dunno, but she ottta know by nahw ah got gud kids, and dat dayed be back, Ah just need the pirogue te fish today."

''Nahw, yu hare whut Ahm sayin' bout de wada? Nah yo on go on git on outta har so ah can finish dis gumbo. And don't go far. Don' go outta da Bayou Allemands, yu har me? Stay outta de lake. The wada is too choppy!"

"Yes, ma'am," and he kissed her gently goodbye.

Donnie, Glen and Earl ran by on their way to check the traps.

"Stop runnin' in de house, boys," their mother told them. Russell mussed Earl's hair on his way out and grabbed his hat from the old deer rack nailed to the wall. He hollered an "Ah will. Stop worrying," to her as he walked out onto the deck of the houseboat. He could feel both in the houseboat and on its deck what his wife was referring to as choppy water. He decided it would be okay if he didn't go far.

So, he stepped into the rocking pirogue, walked unsteadily to the motor and pulled the starter handle. On the second pull the motor came to life. He then chugged his way west into Bayou Allemands.

His wife was right. Redfish love choppy water. A nice sized red hit the line like a ferocious sea trout. It took him a bit to haul it in, but it would make a nice, fresh cubion. Russell decided to try for another one, just out of greed and to occupy what little freezer space they had.

"Ah ha! ah got yu, yu rascal, yu," he said aloud.

4

He felt the brisk breeze blowing harder and then become gale force. It started to pour down rain in sheets, accompanied by thunder and lightning. He hurried to his motor, rocking with the boat. Russell had to stand to get any leverage on the pull cord, lost his balance and fell into the Bayou. Since he didn't have the boat secured with an anchor, it moved, and he couldn't catch it. Normally Bayou Allemands wasn't deep, but where he was it was over his head. Russell was a good swimmer, but the wind and the waves got the better of him. He went down after fighting for his life and never came up again.

Back home the boathouse was rocking badly. Sible was scared, as were the

children. "Wunda whar dat Papa o' yurs is?" she asked. "He can't be fishin' in a hurricane

Dat'whut dis is, in't it, Donnie? A hurricane? I sar yu on yar short wave radio a bit ago."

"It in't a big one, Mama," he said. "It went in at Huoma" He hadn't told her because he didn't want her worrying.

"Well, it feels big to a fambly livin' on the wada wit a husband out fishin'," she said.

"How fas is de wind blowin'?"

"A 100 mph," he replied, "which in't a whole lot fer a hurricane."

"Yu go see if yu can stand still on the deck," she said looking at him in the eyes. He pulled a face, which obviously meant no thank you.

"Mama, will Papa be otay?" asked Kitten, their youngest.

"Yes, Bebe. Nahw yu and Shelly go play wit yore dollies fer nah. Let Mama do de worryin';" she hugged her and pushed her gently over to Shelly.

But, Papa wouldn't be okay. They found his body all the way upstream of Des Allemand,

washed up at Baie Deux Des Chennes. "Pretty powerful wind to push someone that many

miles upstream," the coroner said. In fact, among all the 1.5 million dollars of material

devastation the unnamed hurricane caused, Russel Thibodaux was the only fatality. The storm had gone on to wreck the boathouse he had built for his family, forcing them out along with the others of Bayou Gauche. The boathouse completely sank and the rentals were torn to dilapidated shreds.

Nobody on Bayou Gauche got one red cent from Sydney Simoneaux. They all became homeless and relied on the state and Red Cross for food and shelter. The little bit of cash Sible could grab before the boathouse went down was next to nothing. While their mother and sisters slept on cots somethingn a school building and ate what they were served, the boys continued to trap and sell their pelts. Were their papa living, thcy could save the meat, too. But, for their mother to cook the meat, she'd have to have a stove and pot, and they'd need to have another roof over their heads. Maybe, in time, they would have the money to buy a tent, a cook stove, and a pot. *Maybe,* they thought. *Just maybe. Then they could weave some crawfish nets together, too.*

By the time the coroner finally released their papa's body, their mother had cried all the tears she could spare without becoming a corpse herself. *Ah need to hep ma chirrun*, she thought. So she held herself together for them. A little money came in from the sugar cane relatives in Abbeville, but they had much preferred Sible and her kids come live with them. Money was hard to come by, but having a job in the sugar cane fields was much more in demand. *Russell wanted his fambly har,* she told herself.

Sible was a beautiful, tiny girl when she married Russell. She was a sixteen-year-old, pious, thing, who didn't believe in fooling around until after her marriage vows, much to Russell's chagrin. But, Donnie was conceived just six months later, then

Glenn followed two years after him, Earl three years after Glenn, Shelly, six years after Earl and Kitten, the baby, three years after Shelly. Russell had spaced out their children pretty well for a couple following the withdrawal method. Sible was glad about that so she didn't have to worry like some women did whose husbands drank. And, she kept herself up pretty well for a widow with five children.

After Russell's wake, men didn't have enough respect for her privacy before pursuing her again. Mr. Boudreaux came to the school gymnasium in search of her cot, for example.

"No tank yu, Mr. Boudreaux," she told him "Ahm not ineresed at all."

The boys meanwhile were still going out to bait the traps in the morning, but weren't getting anything in the evenings because of the weather, So, they decided to salvage used boards from the pile of wood damaged by the hurricane, that, and used nails they ripped from those boards to reconnect them.

"Hey, Earl, grab me one of dose boards ova der, will yu?" asked Donnie.

"Shore, Donnie," Earl answered, and handed Donnie the board.

"Gimme dat one, too, so ah can git the nails off it." Donnie added.

"Wit what?" Earl asked him.

"Wit dat crow bar laying on the ground der."

"Oh, ah didn' see dat, no. Hahw did yu know it was der?" Earl asked.

"Ah sar it when we walked ova har," Donnie told him. Glenn was just grabbing boards and throwing them into a pile.

"Trow the ones wit de nails on em on dis pile, Glenn." Donnie ordered.

"Yu got it, bro," Glenn answered.

"Hey, yu boys, whatcha doin' ova der?" A friendly man about their dad's age asked them.

They told him what they were doing and why.

"Mai, ah tink we can hep each udder, yeh," he said. So he came over to where the boys were working to discuss a deal with them.

"Ah'll first hep yu build yore houseboat den yu can hep me build ma house back," he suggested.

The boys thought that was a great idea, since they'd need an adult to oversee the boat part of it so their mom wouldn't worry about it sinking.

When they hit the gymnasium door, they were starving and dove into their evening meal their mama always saved for them form the Red Cross' offering.

When they came up for air, they told their mother the good news. It was always their older brother's place to speak to their parents first.

"Der was a man who want to hep us build back our boathouse," Donnie said.

She looked at him skeptically. "Whut far?" she asked.

"Whut do yu mean whut far?" he asked.

"When people do something far yu, dars always a whut far," she said.

"Oh dat." Donie continued. "As a tradeoff. He heps us rebuild our boathouse, and den we hep him rebuild his house."

"And, whuts' this fellas' name?" she asked.

"Broussard." Donnie said. "Gaspard Broussard."

It was almost like he hit a long-forgotten nerve, because, suddenly, his mama's eyes became the size of saucers. *Shorely dis can' be ma Gaspard Broussard,* she wondered. *My Gaspard should be an archbishop by nahw. At de vary least a bishop or Monsignor.*

"Whut's de matter, Mama?" Donnie asked.

"Oh, nutting, Chere. Ah just felt a ghost run ova yore papa's grave."

10

The boys just sat there looking at one another. Sible turned and tucked the covers under a sleeping Kitten.

All night long Sible slept fitfully. She couldn't sleep until she knew if this was *her* Gaspard Broussard. In the morning while her boys were dressing for work, she said: "Ahm gonna walk yu lunch to yu today."

Glenn asked, "Yu tink dey can give us sumting udder dan peanut butta and jelly sanwiches?"

"No, Chere, I tink dey give us whut dey can. We don' have no choice."

Glenn hung his head and shook it. She rubbed his back. "It won' be foreva, Bebe."

At noon, Sible and her girls walked to the scene of the damaged houseboat and buildings. She was surprised by how nervous she was. When she saw him her knees buckles. She paused, then she walked on. When he looked up, he had the same reaction. He could barely speak, but he made himself say her name.

"Sible?"

She returned his greeting. "Gaspard."

"Hahw?"

She answered him with "Yore workin' wit ma boys."

You could tell he wanted to look at them, for they were looking at him, but he just couldn' take his eyes off of her. He was afraid she would vanish into thin air.

"Yu still unattached 'cept fer God?" She asked hin.

He nodded, still captivated by the shock of her presence.

She handed the boys their lunch, told the girls not to go near the water then sat down near Gaspard to learn how he came to Bayou Gauche without his clerical collar. He learned her story and she learned he'd been in the seminary only for about a year before his dad was killed working on the railroad. She knew he was an only child so he had to leave the priesthood before his vows to care for his mama. She lived in one of Mr. Simoneaux's houses. He was driving from New Orleans to Bayou Gauche once a week to take her to into Houston for cancer treatment.

"It's a wunda we haven' run into one annuter before," he said.

"It is a wunda, but ahm glad," she said, "becuz nahw ah can follow ma heart."

He smiled at her and reached for her hand. She place her other hand lovingly on the side of his face.

"Ah still love yu afta all dis tahm," she said.

"And ah do you, too, Sible, God notwithstanding," he replied. "Ah want yu to cum live wit me at ma house in N'Orlean, Sible. Ah don' want yu and your fambly to be beholdin' to the Red Cross, anymore. Yu all can live wit me and my mama, and ah don' want to hear anutter ting about it."

Sible just smiled, saluted and said, "Yes, sir."

And just like that she was where she wanted to be most in this world

That night, when they were packing their clothes and possessions in the paper bags they had packed them in to come to the gymnasium, Shelly, her most precocious child, asked her if she really loved her papa.

"Oh, yes, Sweethart," Sible answered her.

`The boys were stuffing their clothes in their bags but listening in.

"But, luv is a complicated ting. Yu see, Gaspard and ah were yong when we grew attracted to one anutter. But, ah knew he wanted to go into the priesthood, and ah defended his right to do so. It was a divine calling, and ah had no business interfering wit dat, Still, ah missed him and had no idea he had left the priesthood. Might it have made a difference? Yes, it might have, but by den ah had fallen in luv wit yore papa, so ahm happy ah have all of yu to remind me how happy ah was wit him."

After hearing her out, all the boys, but Donnie, and Shelly gave her a hug.

"We are happy fer yu dat yu will have a new luv and a new life," Shelly told her.

Kitten just looked on. "Whud was all dat bout?" she asked.

The next morning after their Red Cross oatmeal, the family met Gaspard out the door and climbed into his 1920 Posterazzi Ford Model T Touring car.

"Oh, man," said Glenn, "Ah shore tink our luck has changed far de betta." Donnie nudged him.

"Whut's de matta?" Glenn asked him. Gaspard went around to help their mama with the bags.

"Jus keep it quite on de way up dar," Donnie told him.

"Don' worry, ahm enjoyin' dis ride, too much." Glenn smiled and leaned back.

"Guess we're not workin, tday, huh?" asked Earl.

"Yu want to?" asked Glenn.

By this time Gaspard and his mother were back in the car.

"Dis is a nice car, Gaspard. Ah know the Church didn't pay far it."

He laughed. "No ma'am, Dad's life insurance did."

"Oh, ahm sorry ah asked."

"No, nahw, Sible, Ah don't want yu to be sayin' dat 'bout everythin' dat's new to yu."

"Here's one ah know ah'll ask yu," she said.

"Whut's dat?"

"Whut order did yu go into?"

"Mais, dat's an easy one. Yu know hahw ah luv to teach? Well, ah went into the Dominican Order."

She smiled. "Dat makes sense, and, yu know, dat's de one in ma mind ah had yu go into."

He just looked at her and smiled, then, took her hand while he was driving.

For the most part Sible's kids were feeling they were so happy to see their mom get a new lease on life. If any of them were jealous, it was Donnie. He didn't know exactly what he was feeling, but he wanted to think it was a kind support for his papa.

Once they reached Gaspard's home; they saw it was a lovely brick building like every other brick building in the neighborhood. They entered the front door after a secret knock that Gaspard had told his mother he would use so she would know it was him. It was a loud knock, because she was hard of hearing. Then he let himself in. She was an old woman sitting in a chair in the living room covered with a blanket listening to an older radio on a stand. She made to stand up. Sible noticed and told her in a louder than normal voice:

"Oh, no, keep yore seat, please ma'am.:"

"Mama. Dis is Sible. The lady ah told yu abut yesterday," he said. She looked like she was searching her memory.

"Yu remember? Frum my old grammar schul?"

"Oh," she said "yu find har! Will we be haven a weddin' nahw?"

Sible looked down embarrassed. Gaspard was nonplussed. Sible looked at him and smiled. He told her when they were putting their things away upstairs that "Yu know hahw old ladies can be. Very forgetful, yet they remember tings frum the past meticulously."

"Oh," Sible said, "did yu talk abut marrying me in the past?"

He put his head down then looked her in the eyes.

"Yes," he admitted. They were alone, so he took advantage of it, leaned over and kissed her.

She grew heady; his lips were sweet. When they looked up Donnie was standing looking at them.

"Ahm sorry, Donnie. Ah thought we were alone," said Gaspard.

Donnie swallowed his rage and left the room.

"Whut was dat about?" Gaspartd asked Sible.

"Yu don't shuld worry bout it. Ah'll handle it."

"But we have to work togetha tomorra," he sat down on the bed.

She took his hands. "Ahl handle it tonight," she said.

"Okay. Supper's at 7:00," he said as they parted.

When she left her room, Sible walked directly to her boys' room, where she found all three of them sitting there with Donnie talking in whispers. She was sure she knew what he was whispering to them about.

"Donnie," she said, "Ah want to talk to yu." When the others got up to leave," she said to them, "stay. I may as well talk to all of you about dis, too. Ah want yu all to know dat when ah met yore papa ah was sixteen years old. Dat would be old enough to know ah was in luv. When ah met Gaspard. ah was only thirteen, and had developed only a crush on him, but a crush is not the same ting as falling in luv. When ah had to let Gaspard go, Ah was fourteen, only a yar yonger dan yu are nahw are now, Donnie. Now, ah don' tink yu would know if yu are in luv with anyone right nahw?

"Yuck," he said.

"Yu see. When yu are in luv wit someone yu certainly wuldn't say 'yuck."

He looked away. "People are different. Boys and girls are different. A boy wuld need to be older dan a girl 'fore he knew he wuld be in luv normally, and vice versa. Nahw, ah knew ah had a crush on Gaspard, but didn't allahw it to grow into luv until your papa was gone. Surely if he weren't gone, ah wuld have kept on luvin' him, and his presence would have made it so. So please don't continu to punish Gaspard for bein' nuting but a gud and Godly man, and one who is devoted to making our lives betta ones. Supper is at 7:00," she told them, then turned to go out.

When supper started Sible was in the kitchen with Gaspard finishing the meal. Gaspard always did the cooking for his mother. In fact when he wasn't with her, she always had frozen food he had cooked for her ahead of time and stacked in her freezer so she'd had supper waiting for her in her microwave every day. Today was special. They wouldn't be keeping left overs for microwaveable meals today.

Donnie waited for his mother to leave the kitchen and take something to the table to slip in and speak to Gaspard

"Mr. Broussard, ah just wanted to apologize to yu 'bout ma attitude yesterday. Ah really appreciate whut yu are doin' fer ma fambly. Ahm lookin' forward to workin' wit yu." Then, Donnie shook his hand.

When Sible came back into the kitchen she had crossed paths with Donnie on his way out. She looked him all the way to his seat, but he never looked up. When she turned to Gaspard he looked like some visitor from outer space just came down. He looked over at Sible and asked:

"Whut culd yu have said to him in dat short amount of tahm dat culd o' generated an apology?"

"Ne'er underestimate the powa of a muther," she said and kissed his cheek.

Although they were sleeping in strange beds, they were no stranger than their houseboat beds were to start with, so they could adjust. These beds were also strange but very restful, and they sure beat the heck out of the Red Cross cots, though they were, indeed grateful for them. Like the Godly man he was,

Gaspard said grace before breakfast, just as he had said grace before supper.

During his drive to Bayou Gauche, Gaspard asked the boys about their interests. The boys waited for Donnie to speak first, but he never said a thing. Gaspard then said:

"Wait. wait, ya'll, don' hit me all at once. Wait yore turn."

The boys weren't sure what just happened.

"Ohhh. Yu got a sense of humor," Donnie remarked, and the three boys laughed.

"Gaspard came back with, "Gimme sum credit for tryin'.""

Before it was over, they were all singing old tunes from the radio, then they started discussing their papa's designs on the boathouse, which Gaspard said he'd like to recreate their father's design for the boathouse exactly. That excited them.

Back at his house Sible quietly slipped out of the room without waking the sleeping girls. She found Mrs. Broussard asleep on the chaise. She pulled her blanket over her chest, but she opened her eyes.

"Oh, pardonnez moi, Madam," (Oh, pardon me, Madam) Sible responded.

"Je ne dormais pas. (I wasn't asleep) the old woman said and pulled herself to more of a sitting position)

"Bonjour, Madam Broussard. S'il te plait, prends juste un café avec moi?" Siible smiled at her. (Morning, madam Broussard. Will you please have some coffee with me?"

"Mai oui," (Well, yes) the old woman smiled back.

"As-tu bien dormi sur cette chaise?" (Do you sleep well in that chair?)

"Oui, Je dors dessus toutes les nuits." (Yes. I sleep in it every night)

Sible's girls got up rubbing their eyes,

"Mama, I'm hongry."

"Ah mon sha 'tite Bebes." The old lady acknowledged them.

Sible pulled both girls to her and said, "Good morin', Bebes, cum nahw, let's go get sum brekfas'," and she took them into the kitchen for the left-over bacon and for fresh eggs and toast. She put the coffee pot to heat on the stove as well.

She hollered to the old lady: "J'ai trouve des ecrevisses dan congelatuer. Que desir te un etouffee aujourd'hui? (I found some crawfish in the freezer. Would you like some etouffee today?) Sible asked the old lady.

"Oh, mais oui, ne te donne pas la peine." (Oh, yes, but don't go to any trouble) She replied.

"Ce n'est pas un probleme," (It's no problem) Sible hollered back.

By the time Gaspard and the boys got home it was 7:00. Donnie and Glenn fell through the door, while Gaspard carried the sleeping Earl.

"Sorry we're late," he told Sible. "Umm, what's that delicious smell?"

"Dat's my Mama's etouffee," Donnie told him.

"What happened?" she asked looking at Earl. Then she looked at Gaspard for an explanation. He shrugged his shoulders. "Dat's tru." he said.

"Oh poor bebe," she said. "Go put him in bed, Gaspard,"

"Not without a showa and supper," he said.

"But he's only ten." she defended him.

"He'll feel much betta wit a showa and supper," he countered.

She looked at him as though she could feel their first argument brewing, but she wouldn't challenge him in public. So Gaspard went into his bathroom for a shower while the boys went into the larger bathroom to clean up. Sible helped Earl wash up, he was so sleepy, then they all came to the supper table. Before each of them sat a bowl of rice and etouffee with a side dish of potato salad. Their mouths watered. It was all they could do to wait for the short grace Gaspard said before digging in. The boys had yet another serving with ice tea before they crashed,

Once Sible got the girls in bed, she went to Gaspard's room to talk to him. His mother was sleeping in the living room so that part of the house was out of the question. She knocked gently, and was told to come in. He was already in bed with his pajamas on, but he sat up with her on the end of it.

"Gaspard, we need to tawk." she said. "Dese are ma chirrun." she confirmed.

"Ah know dat, Cherie," he replied,'

"Den, when ah say put Earl in bed, wha don' yu?"

Gaspard hung his head. "A don' shuld have kept de boys out dat late. Dats ma fault, Frum nahw on ah won' be late for suppa. De boys will feel betta clean and full in de morning, Please forgive me."

Her heart melted.

"Listen Sible, Ah want us to git married. Ah luv yu and ah luv yore kids. Ah feel like ah waited long euff, and ah don' want to wait no more," he told her.

She felt the same, but she wanted to wait a little longer in case another issue with the kids came up, so she put him off by telling him she wanted him to take the time to decide whether he wanted a child of his own. Besides, she hadn't waited like he did. She had fallen in love in that tine and had a loving marriage and kids in whom she saw the man she loved every day in her growing boys. She saw him most in Donnie. Donnie was built like him, had blue eyes, shaggy brown hair and the most beautiful dimples, *Lordy, those dimples* she thought. She sure missed them. Only time would tell her about Gaspard, though.

Fortunately, things improved. The boys were home by 5:00, and they were never worn out again. About a month later, when they home after work, it was:

"Oh, Mama, you shuld see whut we dun wit de houseboat!!"

"Really?" asked Sible

"Yes," said Donnie, "Papa wuld be so proud."

She looked at Gaspard,

"Ah tink he wud be," and he smiled widely.

able thought: *ah tink its tahm we have dat sarios tahk nahw*

Sible agreed to marry, and planned a big church wedding, which she didn't have for her first marriage. It came with picking out colors, flowers, a cake, and the whole nine yards, Gaspard didn't spare any expense. Russell thought it a needless expense.

The next Saturday she had the boys look after the girls so they could go look for their rings; it should have been a warning sign to Sible, but she wrote it off to passion. Once Gaspard had her alone in the car, and they had picked out their rings, he gave her the deepest kiss yet. She couldn't say she didn't like it, because she did. But he didn't stop there. He wanted more. Far more than Russell had wanted at this time in their coming marriage. He had her pinned against the back rest and kept whispering,

"Come on, Bebe, we're almost married."

It was hard for her to push him off, because he was a bigger man than Russell.

"Are yu a couillon? Yu jus came out of the seminary, and yu act like dis?! Not even Russell pushed me dis far!"

He apologized. She rearranged her clothes and they drove back to his house.

A month later, at the church, Donnie was Gaspard's best man, Shelly, the maid of honor, and Kitten, the ring bearer. As the priest was reading their vows, which they would repeat after him, he asked, "if there was anyone who would have any reason to contest this marriage?" You could see Gaspard start to sweat. Then a woman stood up to challenge it.

She said that "she and Gaspard were lovers, and that he told her he was helping out a family going through some hard times because of the hurricane. She didn't know he was planning to marry one of them." You could have heard a pin drop, though there was a gasp or two.

Every ounce of blood drained from Gaspard's face, Sible quickly looked up at him and asked "if it were true?"

He tried to explain, "Sible, that was before --"

She put her hand up. "Is it true?" How could he say no with Suzette seated right out in the congregation? He nodded his head. Sible had Kitten bring up the rings. When she tried to civilly give them back to him, and he didn't take them, she let them drop to the floor. Sible then turned on her heels, and threw Shelly's bouquet in his face,

Sible camly walked down the aisle she had just walked up, stopped at the intruder's pew and faced her. "May ah please ask you name?" Sible inquired.

"Suzette Devereaux," she said, her head held high.

"Tank yu, Suzette. Yu jus kept me frum makin' the bigges mistake of ma lahfe." Sible then walked out of the church, completely humiliated. Her kids followed one by one. They hitched a ride to Gaspard's with one of his relatives to pack their bags, and then wait for him to take them to their new boathouse. She knew she had a lot of explaining to do, which she wasn't looking forward to, but she never lied to her kids, and she wouldn't start now.

After she got Gaspard's pleading out of her hair, then talked to the kids about how wrong she was about what 'a man of God' is, they got down to business. Since the wayward wedding was supposed to be held in June, the kids had a three-month reprieve from school. And, in that time, Sible started making the ticking they'd need for mattresses. Shelly turned out to be a quick learner so she helped a lot with that, while the boys started to build a pirogue to help them trap and fish. They'd also need help getting past he anniversary of their papa's death when school started in September. Sible didn't know how even she could get past it herself, yet.

"Mama," Glenn said one morning after checking last night's trot lines, "I caught a turtle. Ahm really upset bout dat cuz yu know ah don' lahke hurtin' turtles,"

"Ah know, Bebe," she answered and she kept right on stitching." But, we reala need sum food on de table. Kneel down and tank de turtle, den tank God an do whut yu hav to do," she said, and rubbed his back, hoping to make him feel better." Ahm goin' to make us sum gud turtle soup wit it tonahght," she said. His body language told her how disappointed he was for having to kill it, but it was very difficult to save the life of a turtle who swallowed a whole chicken leg that was sitting sideways in its neck; the bait was set for a garfish or crab, but the turtle took it instead. He wished bait came with instructions. Sible went back to work with her ticking.

Donnie came in to see his mama and told her the pirogue was ready, so Earl was ready to go back to school in the fall. "Mrs. Perygene will be happy with dat," he smiled and wiped the sweat form his face and his neck. Donnie had just had a birthday in July and spent yesterday with his first girlfriend.

"Hey, Mama. Can ah tahk witchu a minit?"

"Shore," she said, and went on stitching.

"Well, yu know ah sar Betty Sue yesteday?"

"Yes," she said. "Hahw did dat go?"

He hung his head. "Ah don' know hahw to ask ma mama bout someting ah should be askin' ma papa." he said.

"Ahm sorry, Donnie, but ahm it," she said, and put her stitching away to give him her undivided attention.

"Whut do yu need to tell me, Donnie?"

"Yu know when yu said dat Gaspard had pushed yu like he did in de car? Well, whut if it was de utter way 'round?"

She knit her brows. "Hahw do yu mean, sun?" she asked him

"Well, um, ah mean she grabbed ma worm," He said, but his eyes wouldn't meet his mother's.

'When she realized what he met, she broke out laughing.

"Mama!" he said, "dat's not funny?"

"A course it's not Donnie, cept to hear it de utter way 'round. Well yu tell her dat's not vary Christun of her. Nahw y'all git in that pirogue an get us sum fish!" she ordered him. "Dig us sum worms quik," and she pointed at the dirt. Donnie was very disappointed that's all his mother had to say about it. He was sure his papa would have said much more. But, as she said, "Ahm it."

Meanwhile, Shelly had skipped in with her ticking. "Mama, ahm ah doin' dis rahght? I dunno."

"Yes, Sha, yu are doin' it rahght. Just continu in dis lahne and yu'll do jus fahn."

Kitten then ran in with her own stitching and bedding to ask her mama's advice.

"Oh, Bebe, dat is jus fahn, too, yeh. Ah tink yu are doin' so gud." Kitten smiled and loved on her mama.

That, along with following Russell's advice, about fishing and trapping what they could off the land, helped them remain completely off the grid and to stay busy. It also helped them enormously saving what little they got from their pelts. Maybe someday they would feel knowledgeable enough to build a shrimper like papa and add shrimp and crab to their catch. At dark, they would all turn in, and save yet more money. Maybe someday they could afford something for the gas lanterns. Russell wouldn't have been prouder of his family.

In time, Donnie would marry Betty Sue Ramirez, Glenn, Inez Roberchoate, and Earl, Cat Lege. Shelly would begin to date an LSU football player named Billy Chatigneu. By this time Sible had been made a Mon Mon by Donnie and Betty Sue's first born,

Ducette, and they all still lived off the land and sea, only with more houseboats, like papa would have liked his extended family to do. Living off the grid turned out to be a nice fit during the Great Depression, too. And, no one would be jumping out of the houseboat, either, unless they were going for a swim.

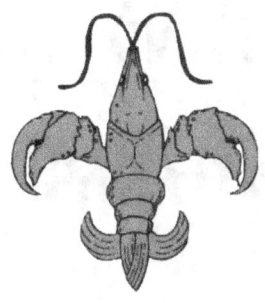

Emile Clama and the Atchafalaya

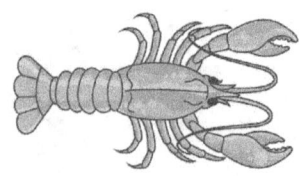

EMILE CLAMA & THE ATCHAFALAYA

Joostain Wilson, the comic and Cajun chef, and one of his former four wives were blessed with one son. They named him Harry D. II, which turned out to be too staid for Joostain, so he called him Emile Clama instead. Here's his story as told from Joostain himself: Emile Clama loved to fish for Sac-a-lait, so he often brought himself up above the northern part of the Atchafalaya River whar the wada was fresh. Atchafalaya was a Choctaw word which meant long river, an' ah gha rawn tee, it was. It starts in St. Mary's Parish just above the brackish Basin whar de Wax River joined it afore dey bot flowed into the Gulf of Mexico. Den, when the wada level was just right, like a gud Cajaun, Emile Clama wud fish fo hours trying like hell, yeh, to get his limit o'Sac-a-lait. An, if he didn't, no, he wuld boudé all day long, puave bête. One tahm one o' dem, how you say it? Men what wears a mask ova his face and dives in de wada for fun? He say he do it tre or two tahms a mont. Anyway, Emile been fightin diss beast of a

Sac-a-lait for tirty minutes, because we pure bleed Cajauns take our fishin real cereal.

"Ah tinks ah must o snag ma lahn wit a tree," Emile him saids,

De man wit de mask sees dat Emile Clama is snagged alright, but it's to a treasure chest of gold coins. Suddenly, down in he wada he sees dat lahn go slak, yeh. And back den we don't have no GSP, no, so puavre Emile, he'd have to drag de whole rivesr to find it again. Den dar was de tahm he caught so many bream fishing in his fran's boat, dat he tells his fran, "it's too bad we can't mark dis place." His friend tolds him that he could, and tooks his knife and cut a mark on de side o de boat, which Emile didn't see. Ahm sure Emile would have told him that's no betta, no. De nex tahm his fran takes him, and Emile saids, "Let's go to dat spot we fish at afore."

His fran saids "Oh, I'm sorry, Emile. Ah borrowed dis boat from my udder fran and it's not mark on dis boat, no."

In tahm, Emile makes marriage wit a female women girl from Crowley name o Ida Babineaux. She her was workin in a town way up nort in Shrevport in de Silver Service up der. Together dey make der first chirren an name him T-Louis. Emile was so happy, yeh, dat he finally have a boy to fish wit him. But, Ida puts her foots downward and wudn't lets de boy go on de wada wit Emile til he was older. When T-Louis was ten or nine, Emile tell him to go get that, quelquechose what would hep him to float if he fall in de wada. When T-Louis comes back wit his life jacket, Emile smile and saids, dats it, yeh, so dey load de boat wit lines, tackle and a bucket of minnets and head out. Life was finally gud for Emile.

De first place Emile Clama take his boy is right around the place he had once get dat snag in case T-Louis him could to catch dat big Sac-a-lait. He tooks him as closes as he guessed he was to dat snag. Shore, enuff, in fifteen or ten minutes, T-Louis gots dat snag him, too, yeh. Emile gots so excited he wets his pants. At first it snag real hard, den it starts to came loose wit de pull like a water-logged bag of flour. In tahm dey pull up someting like a light blue tarp wrapped round someting like boudain. But, when dey look inside, hoo! It smell bad, yeh! Dat's when dey realize dey have a peoples in de tarp!! Pooyie, but dey have to drag dat tarp and peoples all de way in to de boat ramp, so de police mans can see it, cuz dey have no way to mark whar dat is, no. But de most of de problem is dey miss de whole day to fish. Before long de suspect falls on Emile.

But, Emile, him say, "if ah did dat, yeh, why would ah go out dar, and brought it back_to the police mans?"

Dey say, "because yore son hooked it, and chu didn't want to disappoint him if it was a big fish."

Hoo, but Emile, him, was hot! Dey put him in the petroleum car and brought him to de policeman's station. Dey put his son in anudder petroleum car and brought him home to Ida. Emile Clama had his wet pants, too, and he couldn't s'plain dat, no. Dat would jus git him in more trouble, yeh. At de police station, dey put him in a little room, and make him wait. At dat tahm. yeh, he finds la porte de l'arrier, and makes for his escape. He hitch a ride to de boat launch to gots his truck. From dere, he calls de coroner, a fishin buddy.

Emile he axes him, "What's de DI of de dead peoples in de blue tarp?"

De coroner him saids. "De old womans is Olite LeBlance from Abbeville."

Den Emile ax, "What she dies of?"

He saids, "natural causes."

Emile Clama drives all de way to Abbeville to clear out his name, yeh, so he cuds go fishin again. Her fambly saids dey cudn't paid for a funeral and dey cudn't paid to cook her neither, no. So, dey jus dump her in de Atchafalaya. Wit dat fomation Emile drive back to de police station. Dey saids dat he is an escaped prisoner anyhow. Emile's eyes roll, yeh. *Pauvre le Emile.*

De next moning, Emile is hot, yeh. He's so damn hot his morning couche couche turns to cayenne afor it hits his mout. Steam comes outta his ears, ah gha rawn tee! An the fire in Ida's eyes was just as bad, yeh, when she bail him out at $5,000. Hoo, but dat's a lot of money, yeh, and den she tolds him she hads to mortgage his truck for dat! She was hotter dan a wet hen what had all her eggs eat up by a chicken snake. He gots even hotter. Still, de first ting he done was go home and gots T-Louis to go fishin. He tooks dat mortgaged truck and launched his boat in the Atchafalaya looking for Sac-a -lait. He brought some minnets an a bottle of dat, whut you call, Jacque Dan yel, behind Ida's back cuz she wouldn't have approve of dat, no. He told T-Louis it was a special sauce dat would make de fish bite more betta. But when he poured de whole bottle in wit de minnets dey didn't swim likc demselves, no. And, dey fights de hook, hoo, but dey fights dat hook.

So Emile he saids to T-Louis, "Well, guess dese minnets don't like my Jacqu Dan yel. Let's gots some more minnets," and he trow the whole bucket into de wada. Well, when he done dis, yeh, Sac -a - lait start jumping into de boat all de way to de boat launch.

Emile, him saids, "Ah guss dey jus don't want to be hooked. Dey jus works by demselves, yeh." Den, Emile and T-Louis go home where Emile teach his boy how to clean fish.

He tells Ida he know where he gonna made dat money to get his truck outta mortgage. He gonna hads an all -night bourré game wit all his couillon frans, ah gha rawn tee. He's eating his breakfas tellin her dat, yeh, an Gumbeaux jumps up to grab sum bacon out of his plate. Emile kick de dog an it yelp.

Ida say to him, "No need to blame de dog, no."

Emile feel bad. He puts his head down an trows sum bacon on de floor for Gumbeaux, who grabs it up 'fo he can be kicked again, yeh.

Ida tell him, "His frans betta come wit sum pretty deep pockets."

He say, "Don't worry bout der pockets, chu just keep dat strawberry wine comin, and don't give dem nuttin o eat, chu hear?"

So, dat night he invites Etienne, Auguste, Placide and Toussaint to his bourré party.

He tell 'em "Dis is a real cereal game, so y'all come wit deep pockets cuz we will play all night long, yeh,"

Dey say "as long as you gots dat strawberry wine, dats jus fine wit us, yeh." Chu know Emile Clama was knowed wide and far for his strawberry wine, hoo.

Well, at dark, dem mens all sats round de table to pass some tahm wit der fran. Emile starts wit a quarter ante. Dey ahl trow der quarters in wit his, yeh, an den he starts to deal de cards. After everyone gots der five cards, he turns up de trump suit. It's spades. His *couillon* frans starts to drink dat wine, yeh, and Emile, him, he is drinking dat red cool aide. After de udder men have tre or two glasses full, Emile starts to win tricks-mo tricks dan the *couillons* who would by now ante two dolla bills. On der sixth or fifth glass of wine dey were pretty close to laffing at every damn ting, whether dey win a trick or lose it. By de time they were anteing fifty dollars, dey were passing out at de table, ah gha rawn, tee. Emile don't rake in no $5,000, no, but it was pretty damn close, yeh.

"Okay," Ida saids "What yore nex great idea, T-neg? You know, you may as well let dat truck go since your court case is comin' up in 'bout a mont."

"Hell no," Emile saids. "Dats ma truck an ah needs it to go fishin." So Emile Clama tink an he tink bout one udder way to make money, yeh.

One day a fran what owes him some moneys come to his house, and he saids to him:

"Chu knowed dat moneys ah owes chu, yeh? Well ah was jus 'bout to come gave it to chu when sombody robs me."

Emile saids, "how chu let dat happen, Clotilde?"

"He hads a gun." he saids.

"Well chu get chuself a bigger one cuz ah needs dat moneys nahw, yeh."

So Emile he still tinkin while him and T-Louis are fishin for Sac-a-lait.

"Ah got it!" he saids and jump up.

T-Louis he tink his papa gots a big fish, so, he reels in his lahn to grab de net.

"Buts, dats not whats ah mean; ah gots dat udder idea." So, dey fish some more.

T-Louis he saids: "Papa why don't chu soak de minnets in dat special sauce like chu did dat udder day when dey all jump in de boat,?"

"Cuz when dey don't bite dey don't gets to ride, no," saids Emile.

So, when he gots back home he starts boiling crawfishes an crab, yeh. Den he starts to fryin catfishes like he was feedin de peoples Jesus feed who follows Him when he preaches.

Ida saids, "Far goodness sake, Emile, what are chu tinking cookin all dis stuffs?"

He saids, "To pass sumtahm wi ma cou'zas, Abner, Maurice an T-Knock, den to pass de hat." And he smile real big, yeh. "Oh yeh, an chu gots to keep dat strawberry wine comin," he saids to her.

"Chu wants sum, too dis tahm?" she ax him.

"Hell yeh," he saids. "No reason for me to stays sober dis tahm.

"By de end o de mont, Ida had laid out his best blue pin-stiped suit to put on after he shaves, yeh.

And, hoo, but his best cologne, too, dat Old Spittle, dat an his new brown shoes. He was due in court to meet wit his, how do you call it? Prosecutorial lawyer name of Mr. Boudreaux.

Dat Mr.Boudreaux, he saids, "Emile, yeh, brought chuself over har, we gots sum changes to de case."

Emile don't had like dat word changes, no, so he brought himself over to Mr, Boudreaux. Boudreaux saids, "The defendants dey saids you lie bout whats dey saids."

Emile could see all his fears comin true. He wanted to har it anyway. "Dey saids dey would never trow der dearly beloved mama into de lake."

Emile axes, "What's de fine if dey lie?"

Mr. Boudreaux he saids, "$5,000 dollars."

"Ah gha rawn tee dey don't have no $5,000 to pay de fine," he tells Mr. Boudreaux. "I wonder, nahw that the autograph has been premourned; what funeral home do dey want her to go to?"

"I'm not sure what you said. Was that the autopsy and performed?"

"Dats what I saids. "

"Right."

Once de trial began, der was a lot of he saids and dey saids goin on. It continued well until de evenin wit more peoples sayin he saids an onlee one saiyn dey saids. Finally, Mr. Boudreaux ax de peoples if dey coulds pay de fin of $5,000? If not, den how could dey pay de funeral costs of having her buried or cremated? Dey jus sit der an don't say nuttin, no. Prosecuion rests, he saids. De defense didn't have much to add to dat, no. So, de jury wents back to decorate. After tre or two hours dey come back wit a verdit: Emile Clama was innocent!

He accelerate by gettin his truck an Sac-a-lait tackle ready to goes. Den a black fran o his tell him where de Goggleye is bitin like hell, yeh. He thoughts T-Louis mights likes to fish for sumpteen else. So, dey peel a bunch of crawfish for bait an head out down de river til dey gots to dese rocks stickin out o de wada. T-Louis he trows where his papa tell him to an swoop! A goggleye takes dat bait. He starts to reel it in when SLAM! sumtin big hits his lahn.

"Help, papa!" hollers T-Louis, "Ah can't hold did fish, no!"

"Chu doing jus fine, T-Louis, jus hold de lahn an don'try to reel it."

"But papa I'm afraid ah will lose it"

"Don't talk nonsense, chu won't lose it, jus hold on tight to de lahn and let de fish wear hisself out."

Bout dis tahm de fish jumps high outta de wada an tries to spit de hook; he can't do it, no, an he falls back into de wada, but not until T-Louis an his papa see it's about a ten pound bass. T-Louis is so cided, he lets dat bass pull him all round de river afore he starts to reel him in. Emile sits back and smile, ah gha rawn tee!

Bout de tahm T-Louis turns 14 to 13 yars old, he a big scrappin boy, yeh. He eats. Hoo, but dos he eat, jus like all Cajaun boy eats. Dats when Emile Clama makes de decision to take him down to Atchafalaya Basin whar dat wada is brackish. For dose of chu who don't know, brackish wada is a mix of fresh and salt wada. Der are not only mo fish der, but bigger fish, too. The fishes der have mutilated demselves and re climated demselves to dat kind of wada. So, Emile have to taughts he boy how to hook and haul in a garfish, for a sample. Garfish can be real dangerful. Dey have sharp teet, yeh, an can bite chu hand off wit one chomp. Emile tolds T-Louis, in de Basin, dey hads mostly alligator gar, an in the salt water blow de Basin, mostly needle-nose gar.

Alligator gar are good to eat. Hoo, it's good. Ah gha rawn tee it's good. Needle-nose we trow away. But, dey pretty much bite de same, cept neede-nose mostly suck on de bait fo awhile. Kinda like bream do. So, T-Louis and Emile Clama dey preparation demselves and head out, early, early one morning in de A.M. One good ting about garfish is chu can use anyting fo bait, and dey will bite, so Emile started wit ole chicken, tho T-Louia woulds never let much got old in de house. T-Louis, him, started wit stinks bait what they would fish catfish wit. Ever good fisherperson knowed not to use de same ting as de udder fisher person in de boat. Well, de stink baits wins dat tahm cuz T-Louis' line had a hit, WHAM! An his pole bent in two, yeh.

"Papa," he say! "Will ma pole broke?"

"Hell no," his papa say. "You jus keeps a tight lahn on 'em."

Dat alligator pull em all over dat Basin, but T-Louis keeps a tight lahn on him. It tooks him two hours' time to get tire out, bot him an de fish, yeh, but T-Louis was never so proud of nuttin in his lahf. It measures 5'8". Dey could barely git it in de boat, ah ghar rawn tee!

Now, chu peoples what not are Cajauns might not knowed how we Cajauns cook dat alligator gar, yeh, Well, ahm fixin ta tolds chu rat nahw. First, we cut de hide (shell) off all round it. Den, we cut out de part wit le least mount of nerves. Den we cut a line down da middle of dat meat and smother it wit garlic, onions, and lots of our favorite spices. Den we wrap it all up; wit butcher twine, and stick it in de oven where it made its own gravy, yeh. Chu eats dat ova rice, Ah gha rawn tee, but dat is sum gud eatin, bayou style. Whatever chu do, don't try it wit needle-nose gar, no.

One tahm, when T-Louis was 16, dey go fishin Sac-a-lait, dey fill dat fishing basket full, full, yeh. Dose Sac-a-lait dey bent in half dat basket were so full. Since T-Louis he sit in de back of de boat, he was in charge of puttin de basket out and pullin it in. So, when it was full dey knows its tahm to go home. T-Louis, he gots distracts and forgots to pull de basket in. He remembers only when Emile pulls de toggle to speeds up de boat.

"Oh no! He says, "Ah forgots to pull up de basket!" Emile, he let go of de toggle at one tahm.

"You what?" Emile tolds him.

"I forgots to pull up de basket. But, de wada's not deep. I can go in and ge it," saids T-Louis.

"You damn shore will!" answered Emile, "and rat nahw."

When dey gots home Ida she gots so mad at Emile, yeh for making T-Louis go in da wada for to gets dat fish basket and for getting his clothes soaked.. She tolds him he wouldn't get no supper, no. Emile, he gots so hot, he goes out, scales him some Sac-a-lait and fries em up in his outside quelquechose. It's a good ting, ah gha rawn tee, cuz he was practicing for a yar later when him and T-Louis gots stranded in de wada way from shore in de northern part of the Atchafalaya. Dey don't carry no paddles an der battry it wun't start.no. Dey wuz nuttin to do but tie a rope to T-Louis and have him to breast stroke dem in. He did dat, yeh, but it takes him a long time to get back to de launch, ah gha rawn tee. Emile he knew whut Ida woulds say, so him he goes out what to scales him some fish for supper.

But, Ida cames out and said, "Dis tahm was difffernt. You two had no utter way to come in."

T-Louis was so tireds, yeh, he coulds hardly pick up his fork to eat his coubion of Sac-a-lait, no. Emile Clama appoplexed to his son and promised to carry a extra battry from now on.

When T-Louis turned eighteen, Emile had to share his son, not only with school, but with Remy Benoit form Gueydan. Hoo, but he was sweet on her, yeh. He met her at a fais do do.

"Hey, T-Lois, how bout you and me go deep-sea fishin for Red Snapper in Port Aransas?" Emile axed him one night.

"Port Aransas? T-Louis axed. "Ain't dat in Texas?" T-Louis further axed.

"Yeh, but dat won't take none o your gas, no. Ah ll drive," Emile saids.

"Well, dat will take more dan one day, won't it?" T-Louis axed a third question.

"Yes, but we can go on a weekend," Emile tolds him. "Dat red snapper makes a bon coubion."

"Ting is, ah'll have to check wit Remy first. In case she has plans."

"What do you mean 'in case she has plans'?" Emile saids. "Chu'd already know if she has plans. Besides it's red snapper season."

T-Louis he lowers his head.

"Boy," says Emile. "Don't chu let dat girl walks all over chu! Chu want to go somewhar chu go."

48

T-Louis saids, "Ah can'ts hurts her feelings, Papa."

Hrumph," Emile saids and walks away.

T-Louis tinks bout it for a week. He mades Remy mad about it, but he decides to go. "Okay, Papa, Ah'll go."

"Good," his papa says and smiles real big. Dey get their salt water fishing license, some money for the motel and the fishing trip, den packed their bags and headed due east on IH 10.

"I rented a deep wada fishing trip wit Captin Daniel. It's a 6-12 hour trip, so we may have to stay ova for two night," Emile told him when Emile tolds him dat, yeh, T-Louis starts to boudé.

"Ah know nahw dat chu have dat truck, chu don't need to wait for de bus. Ah wanted chu to have it for chur girlfriend. Still, chu don't spend any tahm fishin wit me no mo. Chu will see how much chu will have a good tahm again, yeh, Dis is vary different kinda o fishin. Hell, we can do more of it if it chu lahk it. Nahw chu spend all chu tahm wit Remy an none wit chu papa fishin. Whut ahm tryin to say is ah miss chu, son,"

Still, all the way to Port Aransas T-Louis, him boudé. Him don't want to stay dat long, no, no matter how much Enile tolds him he will hads a good tahm. But when he gots in dat boat and realizes his papa gots it only for dem, his altitude it improve. It's refreshing for him, yeh, to have dat early mornin cool, salt-wada, air blowing in his face, and at first, bouncing for miles on de wada into de Gulf o Mexico. About two miles in, do, he starts to feels sick, yeh. His papa was in de Navy, so he had his sea legs. T-Louis, him had to lean over de boat and trow up de rest o de way. Once der Captin Daniels threaded a large squid onto an 11/0 Mustard 3990 circle hook, an sinks it all de way to de bottom, WHAM! A snapper hits it right away. But, once at der spot, as soon as he drop dat line wit a metal leader an a squid threaded, T-Louis forgots all bout dat sickness, yeh. He foughts and he foughts wit dat fish, hoo, but he foughts for thirty minutes, an when his arm an hand it gets tired, he turn dat rods an reel ova an foughts wit de udder arm an hand. An when he finally pull it in and net it, dat snapper weighed tirty-tree pounds, ah gha rawn tee. Capain Daniel said it calls a Cubera Snapper dat get dat big. T-Louis was 'hooked' him from den on, yeh.

While Emile he fought wit his own snapper, T-Louis has another WHAM! Hit him. But, dis tahm da fish pull more harder,

He axes Captain Daniel, "Can any fishes eats red fishes?"

He says, "Yes, Goliath Grouper. They start at seventy-five pounds and go up from there."

T-Louis knew he had something but couldn't control it.

"Is dis tackle strong enough for a grouper?"

"Plenty strong enough," said Captain Daniel.

Captain Daniel had threaded a whole mackerel with its tail cut off so it'd be rutterless to lure grouper. Dat gave T-Louis de ride o his lahf. It took him tree hours to haul him in an net him. Itweighed close to tree hundred pounds, ah gha rawn tee! T-Louis was never so tired in his life.

Him an papa caught a few more snapper, but de good ting bout it is dey didn't hads to clean em, and he slept all de way in so he never wokes to trow up again.

But. Captain Daniel tolds dem, "keeping de grouper was illegal." So dey tooks a picture of T-Louis holding it de best dat he could den he release it backs into dc wada. Dat was bad since grouper was mighty good to eat. On de way home, T-Louis kept saying,

"Dat was the moistest fun ah'd ever had, even do ma arms are mighty tired, and dat fried crawfish poboy we bought was shore good, too, yeh. Papa, I wish we could do it all again today, yeh."

His papa, him smile real big; his boy was happy fishing wit him again, plus dey were goin home wit an ice box full of snapper filets. It was well worth the cost, as far as money was concerned. He wasn't sure about his time with Ida, yet. Emile sat there in de quiet for a couple of minutes to get what he would say next straight in his head.

"T-Louis, ah been wait 'n to get chu alone to tell chu dat chu mama's not well. No. For tree monts nahw she been havin what chu call dem head acres. So goin to dat female women 's horsepistol to get an MIR dat orincologist ordred for her head. Ahm just hopin it's not a large quelquechose, no."

T-Louis was just about to fall asleep when he realized what his papa was saying. Every bit of the de blood it left his face.

"Oh, no, Papa, not Mama!"

"Well, maybe ahm wrong, yeh, so let's wait til we gots home and see."

When deys gots home, Ida, she say, "Dat doctor she says ah have a tumor de size of a lemon, but it don't look like de cancer kind. Still, she needs to see a new MIR every tree monts."

Emile, him say, "Ah don't like dat, no, Bebe. Let me get Eunice to do de chores for you for awhile."

Ida she don't say nuttin, her, cuz she don't feel good, no. Emile he puts his arm around his wife and holds her tight on de couch for de rest of dey. T-Louis is standing der looking lost. Emile tolds his boy to grab tree of dose fillets and cook em up outside for der supper. T-Louis was glad to hads something to do, yeh.

When T-Louis saw Remy again, and shows her his picture wit de grouper, Remy, she wasn't impressed.

"Dat fish weighed 200 pounds!" T-Louis stares at her. "Well, get used to it because fishing is in ma lah," he told her.

She looked down, thought for a minute and said, "Okay, as long as you remember that dancing is in ma lahf."

T-Louis smiled and asked her, "When's de next fais do do?""

"There's one in Lake Charles tomorrow night," she answered him. He thought about having to drive that far as tired as he still was, but he felt he had no choice.

"Okay, Lake Charless it is." He smiled and put his arm around her. From dat moment on T-Louis had to balance Sac-a-lait fishing wit his papa, caring for his mama and fais do ds wit Remy.

Many tahms after a fais do do he was so sleepy he could hardly hold his pole. One tahm a Sac-a-lait bite wokes him. It was the biggest Sac-a-lait what he's ever hooked. He was just glad that it woke him up cuz it was eleven inches long and three pound!! His papa was begun to be peeved wit him, yeh,

"Son," he saids, "you can't keeps burning de candle at bolt ends, no."

"Well," says T-Louis, "what should I dos, Papa? Remy saids if I wanna fish, she wanna dance."

"Hmph," saids Emile. "You gots youself a qualindry. But, you can always tell her you are helping me wit your Mama. Ida's sister, Eunice, just stayed to help out for de nex tree monts when Ida have to gots dat new MIRs. It showed dat tumor, yeh, had gots bigger, which s'plained why her head acres were getin worser. She had to tooks more and more of dose pills dat doctors give her, Emile, he starts to sell de Sac-a-lait dey catches and den snapper filets he and T-Louis had catched wit Captan

Daniel afore to pay for de horsepistol costs der insurance money didn't pay. And, Emile, he was a good cook, yeh, so he took care of de meals, and T-Louis and Remy de chores. In his spare time, T-Louis fished to sell de Sac-a-lait.

One tahm he had to ax his Papa a question bout a sale. so, he knock on der bedroom door. His Papa say to come in. But, when he did, his papa was holdin his mama, an T-Louis could tell his Papa had been cry; his voice it even crack, too, yeh. Dat broke T-Louis' heart, ah gha rawn tee.

More and more, T-Louis was fishing alone; more and more T-Louis was left to his own devices to make a sale; more and more his Papa would break down and cry right in de middle of supper.

Finally, T-Louis ax his Papa, "Is Mama dyin?"

"I'm scared dat she is, son," his Papa tell him.

It was to de point dat his Papa was cooking her Cream o Wheat for every meal. Most of de tahm, it would remain untouched. Once he helped his Papa take something in der to her, an he was shocked by how much weight she lost. Dats when it finally hit him dat dis is real. He goes to Mama's side o de bed and kneels on de floor by her. At first he don't say nuttin no. He just hads big ole tears run down his face.

"Oh, Mama, chu can't to leave us." He puts his arm around her, leans on ova on her and cry like a baby.

She hold him der and saids, "You'll be alright, T-Louis."

Den, Mama, she puts her hand through T-Louis' hair and don't' say nuttin else.

When he came out of de room, he wiped away his tears and axed his Papa, "Whut'll we do witout her Papa?"

"We'll still love her in har," And he put his fist ova his heart. "But we'll go bout lahf as usual, cuz dats whut she wants," he saids.

And, dats whut dey done, too, yeh. Ten yars afta, Emile Clama and his grandson, T-Pierre, wit his quelquechose on, went fishin for Sac-a-lait in de Atchafalalya. He was gonna sleep ova wit his Grandpere while T-Louis and Remy went dancing at a fais do do in Gran Chanier.

Peggy Marceaux

CULTURE SHOCK

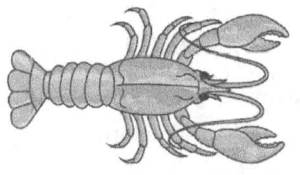

CULTURE SHOCK

circa 1960

Karen was glad her brother-in-law, Travis, had invited them to go on this fishing trip. Mikie missed male companionship and so had she. She nervously checked the temperature gauge on the instrument panel again. *Should have listened to Travis and had the thermostat replaced. At least she wouldn't have had such a hard worrisome three-hour drive.*

"Too late now," she chided herself. "Where is that cutoff to Cameron, Mikie? We must have missed it somehow.'

Mikie continued to stare straight ahead at the road, oblivious to his mother's mutterings. The official Louisiana map did not show the road Travis had advised her to take, and there had been no road signs for miles. She checked the temperature gauge, then the time and panicked. Unless the Gulf of

Mexico appeared miraculously before her in the next fifteen minute, she would miss the 6:00 rendezvous with Travis.

"Where in God's name am I?" Karen glanced quickly over at the five-year-old standing on the seat next to her. She hoped he wouldn't repeat the blasphemy.

His eyes suddenly widened. "Mommy!"

The unannounced hairpin turn took Karen by surprise. She cut the wheel sharply to the left and hit the brakes, but the tires slid over the loose gravel. The rear end of the car swung out, spinning it around twice before flinging it off the road and into a steep ditch.

For nineteen of Karen's twenty-seven years, she had lived alone with her mother. They existed on a cook's salary and the meager tips from the only café in the small East Texas town of Burkeville. Karen felt responsible for the pain that haunted her mother's eyes. She still had trouble dealing with her own illegitimacy, that she was the product of her mother's loneliness in WWII and a soldier stationed nearby.

Culture Shock

One small, black rectangular piece of cloth depicting a heart strangled by a ring of thorns was all she knew of her father. Her mother said it had some religious significance, something about a Catholic scapular he wore around his neck. He called it his heart. She had scoffed, you and his heart. That's all he left me. The rest of the mystery escaped through the frayed end of the cloth. Her mother never married, and Karen resigned herself to being an East Texas nobody, burying her father's "heart" next to her bird, Tweeter, in the back yard. She couldn't even be a bigot or suffer bigotry; she had no particular nationality, subscribed to no particular faith and belonged to no particular political party. She didn't even have a preference for automobile. Back then, she couldn't afford to. History.

Karen let it die. It was Dave who had made her feel alive. A traveling salesman "just passing through." Tough but tender. "Two eggs over easy and a side dish of nails, please." She remembered that sparkle in his blue eyes and the teasing wink that accompanied his order.

How special she felt when he asked her to marry him. As Dave's wife, she had a ready-made identity. Besides a married name, he gave her purpose and self-confidence. His tough side encouraged her to finish business school. His tender side gave her Mikie. Momma and Dave, once all she had in the

60

world. She lost them both last year. Dave to pilot error. Her Mom to a stroke. Now she was so alone and soley responsible for Mikie.

Karen didn't remember slamming into the side of the ditch. She woke to find the front end buckled to the shattered windshield. She pulled herself off the steering wheel, blinking hard, trying to focus. Suddenly, she remembered, but the passenger seat was empty.

"Mikie! Michael?" **Stay calm.** She searched the back seat. *Don't let Mikie stand up in the seat, Strap yourselves in, Karen. Always strap yourselves in.* Dave's word haunted her.

"God, no, **please,** no" The back door was jammed open. Only her rain poncho lay on the back floorboard. Unable to open either front door, Karen crawled into the back and out the door from which Mikie must have been thrown. A sharp pain grabbed at her ribs, but her concern for her son prevailed. Mikie lay unconscious about fifteen yards away. Dark fluid oozed from a huge gash on his forehead. Within seconds, Karen had scooped him up in her arms and wiped the blood from his little eyes.

"Mikie. Mikie!" She shouted. "My God, please no. Please help me!" Frantic she stifled a scream with her bloody hand. She fanned away the hungry mosquitoes and rocked Mikie to and fro, fighting back hysteria,

Stay calm, Karen. Think rationally, don't feel. Think! And suddenly, she realized what she had done. She **moved** Mikie! "What if he had a neck injury? What if he had a back injury? The possibility of hurting him further frightened her even more. Karen wanted to move him to the car, but she was afraid to. She laid him gently back down on the wet grass. The mosquitoes swarmed in the warm July evening. She remembered her poncho, ran to the car and quickly returned to cover the boy. It shielded him from most of the buzzing insects.

She managed to climb out of the ditch without too much difficulty. She knew the road back was barren for miles; her only hope lay in the direction she had been traveling. An anxious glance at Mikie pulled her back to him for only a moment.

*No. Get **tough**. Karen. Get **help**.* She ran on fear for three quarters of a mile, the humidity and ache in her ribs straining her breath. Another hairpin turn. The smell of smoke. She ran faster, searching the overgrowth on both sides of the road for signs of life.

Another forty yards opened onto a clearing. She saw smoke, smelled food, heard voices.

"Help!?" Tears flooded her eyes. "Help me, please. Someone help me!"

In the distance, two men looked up from repairing their nets. She rushed on past two curious mutts.

"Please, help me!"

Three more men, butchering what looked to be a large hog, glanced first at the men repairing the net, then up the road at Karen.

"Hey, gard là bas." One of them raised his chin up in Karen's direction.

"Qui sait là femme?" asked the shortest of the butchers, wiping his bloody knife on his tattered trousers.

"Je n'sais pas," shrugged the youngest. His blue eyes intent on Karen were first skeptical, then curious, then delighted. The short man frowned at the young man's smile.

"Henri," he ordered, *"viens aller Trosclair."*

"Tu vas!" the young man barked back, his gaze disobediently lingering on Karen. Dogs loped

amiably at her side, escorting the wide-eyed stranger into the settlement.

"Can't you people **hear** me? My son is badly hurt." She grabbed the young man's arm and pulled frantically. "Please come. There's been an accident. I need help!" *Henri* allowed Karen to pull him a few feet down the road; he grinned wide, amused by her antics. Karen shouted back at the others. "Please, someone, call an ambulance. And, we'll need more help. Please."

A husky voice shouted down the road after them: *"Henri!"* The young man broke stride and strolled away from Karen. He turned to sneer at the big man who had shouted at him. Karen was confused.

"Please don't stop," she begged the young man. **"Please."**

Henri's eyes never left the big man. He spat in the dirt in front of him then strolled off toward the center of the settlement. Karen's senses came to her long enough to realize that she hadn't understood what these men were saying. She looked fearfully at the big man who turned toward the others.

"Qui sait là femme?"

"Je n'sais pas, Trosclair," shrugged the short one.

"Oh my God! You don't speak English, do you?" she cased the men, shocked. Their eyes blinked back at her then at Trosclair.

"Qu'a l'à a dit?" a tall, lanky one asked *Trosclair*. The big man just waved the question away. He slipped his thumbs inside his suspenders and addressed Karen.

"Sometahm ah spoke it, sometahm ah don'." *Trosclair* stood perfectly still. Only his thumbs moved, tugging at his suspenders, stretching them over his pot belly. Karen sighed

"Um," She tried to take it slow. "Um. Look. Mr.__" *Trosclair* didn't offer. "Well, anyway. I am very concerned about my little...." She paused to keep from choking. "My little boy. We had a very bad accident about a mile down the road. Could you please. Oh, **please** call an ambulance." The tears couldn't be stayed. Her voice cracked. "Mister, I desperately need your help. Please?" No one moved. *Trosclair's* expression remained unchanged, Karen's desperation suddenly exploded into anger.

"What's the matter with all of you? Don't you understand what I'm saying?"

"Wait." *Trosclair* dismissed her and turned back to the men.

He snapped one of his suspenders. *"Odeon!"* Anticipating an order, the short man put his knife into his pocket and stepped forward. *Trosclair* motioned with his fingers toward the camp. *"Vas chez le doctor."*

"Oui," acknowledged *Odeon,* and he scurried off toward the cabins.

Karen was crying now, bewildered, helpless, her arms dangling limp at her side. She knew her son might be dying. They were wasting such precious time. Henri re-appeared. He stepped from behind the men. *"Elle èst très jolie,"* he observed. The other men turned around, frowning at him, displeased. *Trosclair* sliced through him with his black eyes. Henri backed off and shoved his hands deep in his pockets. He smiled at *Trosclair*. The big man turned back to Karen.

"Vien avec moi à mà maison," he invited her, then he turned to lead the way. All but *Henri* followed. She didn't know what had been decided.

"Stop!" she shouted between sobs. *Trosclair* looked back in surprise then slapped the side of his head.

"Oh, mai pardonnèz-moi," he apologized. "Ah forget. Won't you come to ma house, Ladee? Ma frans here will go wit me to git you 'tite gaçon. You don' should worry."

Karen slapped her arms to her sides and threw her head back in absolute frustration.

"No! I will **not!** For Christ's sake!"

Trosclair cringed at her words. "You don't should say dat, Ladee. Shore you goin' to need dat Christ to hep you boy."

She blushed at the admonition, but it cleared her head and let her think again. She spoke firmly to *Trosclair.* "I'm going back. All I ask is that you call an ambulance, and my brother-in-law. His name is Travis Cantrell, and he should be waiting for me at the Seagull Restaurant in Cameron." She choked back more tears and headed back down the road.

"Ladee. We don' have no phone here." She stopped short. *Trosclair* continued. "De closest telephone is in *Grand Chanier* and dat is too far to go today."

The last remnant of Karen's bravery fell to her feet. Heavy sobs transformed into despair. She buried her face in her hands and dropped to her knees.

Trosclair moved towards her. The men followed close behind. "Wait, Ladee, we'll go git your boy." *Trosclair* and *Odeon* each took an arm and lifted her back to her feet. She soon became one in the Cajun

67

crowd that disappeared around the bend. Henri followed just a few steps behind them.

Apparently, there was very little traffic down that road, because the scene of the accident was just as she had left it. Several of the younger men followed Karen to where her son lay. *Trosclair* tried pulling her from the boy, but she jerked away, hovering protectively over her son. Hysteria returned.

"I don't want any of you to touch him, you hear!"

"Qu'a là dit?" asked the young man alarmed by her outburst. Ignored, he shrugged and walked back to examine the car. But, when *Trosclair* cupped his head with one of his big hands, Karen jumped on his back with clenched fists. A tall, lanky clansman was quick to respond. He came up from behind, caught her elbows and pinned them to her waist. Karen screamed louder than before, feeling trapped and sinking into dejection and convulsive sobs.

Trosclair looked back in approval *"Bon, Justin,"* then he returned his attention to the child's heartbeat.

"Ças c'èst petit gaçon," sympathized an old man.

"Oui," agreed *Trosclair* with a smile, pleased with the little thumps he felt against his ear.

Still captive, still sobbing, Karen looked on helplessly as the drama unfolding between the big man and her little boy. *Trosclair* pushed the boy's blood-soaked hair from his forehead. The wound continued to ooze a thick, steady, crimson stream. *Trosclair* pulled a string he had around his neck. A dark fragment of cloth popped out from his long-john shirt. *Trosclair* kissed the cloth and touched it to the boy's forehead. Then, he made the sign of the cross with it and stuffed the little square fragment back into his shirt. He looked back at Karen.

"Jesus will hep you boy, Ladee. Don' you worry, no." Then he turned back to the boy. *"Jean-Louis,"* he called. The fifteen-year-old was at his side in seconds. *Trosclair* made a gesture with his hand over the wound. Instinctively the young buck broke from the Cajun herd.

Karen's fears came to life once more. She squirmed to get free but, Justin held her firmly to him. "Where's he going; what are you going to do?" But only *Henri* paid her any mind. All other eyes were on *Trosclair* and the boy. Henri stepped behind Karen and her captor, interrupting her gaze from the dusty cloud Jean-Louis left behind. Justin was preoccupied, straining to see over *Trosclair's* shoulder. Henri raised an index finger in front of Karen. It moved from side to side with the rhythm of a metronome. His droopy eyes flirted. His breath turned her head.

"Tsk, tsk, tsk, N'fais pas tracasser."

When *Justin* whirled Karen away from Henri, she discovered that *Trosclair* had picked up her son. She panicked, again, kicking to get free. "You leave him alone!" She screamed, then slammed her heel back into the tall man's shin. "Put him down!

"Gaston!" Trosclair commanded.

"Oui!" A heavy man with a long beard stepped forward and slapped Karen sharply across the face. Henri grinned, stirred by the violence.

Stunned, Karen gasped and grew silent. It was a reminder that she was on foreign soil. *Trosclair* faced her warning her sternly with his piercing black eyes. She bowed her head, finally surrendering. No one spoke. All the men joined in her gesture, renewing their acquiescence. All, that is, but Henri.

Jean-Louis broke the tension when he raced back with a hand full of cobwebs. Karen grimaced as she watched him place the dirty mesh on Mikie's bleeding wound. She felt Justin's hands release her, cautiously. She turned away from all of them, rubbing her elbows.

Odeon waited patiently back in the village. He had alerted the women and children to the clansmen's return to the community. Some watched from doorways. Others joined the parade of rescuers proudly accompanying the strange woman and injured child to safety. Dogs ran and tumbled with excitement. The two old women in the center of camp, however, remained near the cast iron kettle. No occasion would be more important than their appointed duty to tend the pot with the crackling hot lard. All other eyes were on *Trosclair,* the boy and Karen, who followed behind like a proper clans-woman now. She became aware, suddenly, of her appearance. She wiped the mascara smeared down her cheeks, seeing for the first time the crusted blood on her blouse, the mud on her legs and skirt. She bumped into *Trosclair* who had stopped just ahead of her. Surprised, she looked up into the face of an old woman—a road map of lines converging into the corners of a sunken mouth. Her eyes looked on at Karen pitifully. *Trosclair* broke the silence.

"Dis is *Taunt Felice.* She will hep you boy." Karen's stomach turned. "You will stay at ma house."

Just at that moment, the cauldron in the middle of camp burst into sizzle; hot lard hissing like a steam

71

engine. Karen's gaze was lured toward the noise, her senses trying to escape, trying to hide themselves from this nightmare. So, for a few seconds, she stood motionless, watching the old women in the distance rake cubes of flesh into the smoking pot. Trosclair waited for her response. It was almost as though he was soliciting it now. Finally, he grew impatient.

"Ladee—?"

"Isn't there somewhere **else** we could go?" Karen interrupted; her eyes remained on the culinary activities in the distance. *Trosclair* looked all around.

"Where, Ladee?" Reality intruded—broke her reverie. She looked him in the eyes; they told her to decide. She turned in a full circle, surveying the tiny settlement. Some three-dozen shack-dwellers watched her study their homes. Like the others, *Trosclair's* house was small. Like the others, there was no sign of paint. Like the others, a little porch jutted out from its doorway like a big lower lip. But, unlike the others, *Troclair's* house merited a small shed. It nestled up to the proud little shanty like an afterthought. Karen mourned its isolation. A riverbed bordered it to the south, tall palmettoes to the east and west. The formidable dirt road that ambushed her and Mikie glanced off its north end. She had no alternative, and *Trosclair* waited for her to admit it. Despondent, she turned back to him, closed her eyes and nodded twice. They ascended to the little porch, shaking playful puppies off their feet.

"Jean-Louis! Ferme à porte" Trosclair shouted.

"Oui," Monsieur," and the door shut just behind the big man, Karen and *Taunt Felice.*

"Qui c'est là femme?" asked a short, fat woman stirring the large pot on a primitive stove. Her toothless gums made a chewing motion. She looked on without much interest. *Trosclair* kicked at the three chickens on the bed. He ignored the woman's question, rifling commands to four children playing cards on the floor. They scampered out the door, shooing the chickens out ahead of them. *Trosclair* called to the woman. *"Inette, le garçon, il èst mal. Taunt Felice vas là aider."*

Her indifference melted into pity. She came forward. *"Bien,"* she nodded, looking with concern first at the boy then at Karen. She smiled. *"N'fais pas tracasser, Chère.*

Trosclair shook his head.

"Elle n'connait pas Français.'

"Non? Umf!" So, she patted Karen's arm reassuringly and waddled past her to one of the tiny beds. *"Couchè le garçon là bas."* She instructed

Trosclair, pointing toward the floor. He obeyed, laying the boy gently on a pallet beside the bed.

At that moment, the door creaked open. Jean-Louis and four puppies bounded in. The spotted puppy had thoroughly bathed Mikie's chin and mouth before Karen could stop it. No words were needed. Jean-Louis and Karen had the puppies up and out of the door before *Trosclair* could say his name. By the time they got back to the one-room dwelling, Trosclair had already moved Mikie to the bed. Felice leaned over the boy, examining the clotted webs.

"Bien," she nodded, pleased with what she saw.

Tosclair nodded back, He turned to Karen. "De blood. It is stop."

Jean-Louis grinned. Karen looked on, concerned but expressionless, afraid to feel relieved. *Inette* nodded at her to console her. *Taunt Felice* pulled a small sack from her bosom, dug deeply into it, and pulled out something small. She handed it to the boy. *"Va chez,"* she said to him, and she rapidly sputtered out some instructions.

Trosclair translated. *"Taunt Felice* wants de boy to bury de nickel under de willow tree on west side of *Gaston's* house."

"What?" Karen was incensed; hoped she misunderstood.

The boy shot out of the house, brushing Henri back just outside of the door. Henri shouted an oath after Jean-Louis and kicked the spotted puppy that pulled at his trousers. The puppy yelped.

Karen felt for the puppy but turned to her son. She kept vigil with *Taunt Felice*. She concentrated on the rise and fall of Mikie's little chest, willing it to keep its rhythm, to keep moving. In the back of her mind she was wondering if Travis had alerted the police yet, wondering when they'd be rescued.

Within minutes the old woman called for another runner. *Trosclair* volunteered his son Raymond. She spoked quickly to him, holding his gaze almost mystically. He grimaced. She repeated the command, more slowly and emphatically. *"Allèz prendre le petite chiens èt apportez-moi le foie!"*

Trosclair looked pathetically on at his boy. Raymond dropped his head, then nodded. Trosclair nudged his shoulder. Without lifting his chin, the boy yielded.

"Oui, Madame."

"Allèz," his father prodded,'

Raymond slipped out of the door, lifted the spotted puppy, and disappeared. *Trosclair* looked up at Karen, as if unsure of what to say. She sensed his discomfort.

"What's going on? What kind of witchcraft are your people practicing here?" She shoved the old women to the side and leaned over to lift Mikie. *Trosclair* quickly aborted an attack of hysteria.

"Ladee, cahm youself down. You will hurt you boy more dan hep him dis way. All Taunt Felice wants to do is to put something on the boys head to hep make it well real fass."

Karen **wanted** to hear those words. She **wanted** to trust *Trosclair*. Back in her world she knew she could get another opinion. But, what did she do in a case like this? What did she do when the rules changed? When an alien culture shocked her instincts impotent. She had to trust in a proxy, she had no choice. She had to rely on the instincts of *Trosclair*. She eased Mikie back down onto the bed, covered his little chest, and retreated.

Inette moved forward to Mikie's head and sponged it gently with warm salt water and kerosene. Karen just stood by and looked on, her face worn by the trauma of the past two hours. The heat started to bother her. Her chest ached. Dusk would be threatening within the hour. Oh please, Travis, hurry. She watched Inette stroke the clotted webs with a wet cloth, soaking them thoroughly. Karen turned to *Trosclair.*

"Where did you learn to speak English?"

"In de city." He measured the curiosity in her eyes. Anticipating more, he concluded: "I live in N'Oleans befor de war. I don' like dat out dahr. Dis is ma home nahw." He turned the tables. "Whatu doin' way out har by youself, Ladee? Who are you really?"

"My name is Karen Cantrell, and I'm **not** by myself." She touched Mikie's arm. She grew defensive. He gave her room. "We had plans to meet my brother-in-law in Cameron. Travis thought Mikie would enjoy a fishing trip."

"Umf! You turned wrong. You just below *Lake Misere,* Ladee."

She caught the irony. It did little for her attitude. She examined *Trosclair's* face, He seemed receptive, after all, he inquired.

"Do many people know about this—this community?"

Inette squealed, the bloody cobwebs had pulled free, leaving the wound clean beneath them. All but Karen smiled approvingly. She wondered what would happen next. She didn't have to wait long.

Karen had never heard of "treating" before. She watched skeptically as *Trosclair* rolled up the tobacco tightly into a cylinder and licked the thin paper to seal it. She watched him light it and inhale it deeply, ritualistically, as he prepared himself for "treating" Mikie. She noted how he had crossed himself, muttering at each end of four points: head, chest, shoulder then shoulder, her eyes widened each time he puffed the smoke into Mikie's ears, first one then the other. "Dis will drive de devil out of his bobo," he assured her. He lowered his head after each puff, holding his breath, his lips moving silently in some French prayer over and over until he could hold that breath no longer. She was enthralled, caught up in the magic of it all. Surrounded by this small collection of primitive marsh dwellers, Karen began to doubt her own sanity. She retreated to find herself again. She needed air. To think clearly. So, she stepped out on the porch, and it helped. Here she could decide whether it was wise to continue to trust *Trosclair's* instincts after all.

As Karen bathed her worries in the sunset just a few minutes longer, a man's arm roughly seized her around the waist. A hand clasped her mouth shut, sealing her terror within. Her eyes screamed her terror as he dragged her into the shed. The door swung freely; tools were knocked about in the scuffle and swallowed in the dimness, then darkness. In a matter of seconds, the man's weight had her pinned against the wall. One hand threatened at her throat while the other pulled at her skirt. There was no doubt what he wanted, but he whispered it just the same, clearer, filthier in French. His foul breath gagged her. His hand fumbled for her underwear. She tried to scream. He clutched tighter, then the door swung open. A large shadow filled the opening. Just as they had imprisoned her, both hands released her. His weight was still heavy against her, but, his gaze was fixed on the doorway, *Trosclair* stared back. Words flew. The attacker shifted toward the big man, motioning him to come nearer. He seemed eager for the fight, his excitement and taunts building the closer *Trosclair* edged. But, before the villain could think to react, *Trosclair* had driven his knee deep into the man's groin. The pain buckled him; he fell to the floor, rolling back and forth in agony. Still frozen in position, Karen saw the man's face in the dim light of the doorway. *Trosclair* kicked twice at his rear before *Henri* could manage to crawl out of the shed. She heard a flurry of strange words, a slap, then the limping of feet fading into the darkness.

Karen was not yet recovered from the grips of fear when *Trosclair* stepped back into the shed. For a long minute, they just stared at one another in the dark. *Trosclair* shifted his weight from one foot to the other. He cleared his throat.

"You okay, Ladee?"

Still trembling, Karen stepped away from the wall and straightened her skirt. She lowered her eyes.

"I've got to get back to my son," her voice quivered. The plea touched *Trosclair*. His voice softened.

"Shore, Ladee. Of cose." He offered her his hand, but she hesitated to take it. Understanding, uncomfortable himself, he stepped out of the shed and turned his back to the doorway. She slipped past him quietly. He would wait for the creak of the screen door.

Karen tripped over the sleeping puppies as she hurried onto the porch. They yelped. She stopped to see if any were hurt, but all seemed fine and accounted for, except for the spotted one. It was noticeably missing. She entered the house and moved toward the bed by lantern light. The coolness of twilight refreshed her, though the close call in the shed still burned on her cheeks. She would ask *Trosclair* what would be done to the man who attacked her. Later. She shivered at the thought of him now. Taunt Felice sat quietly thumbing her rosary beads. Mikie lay still, just as before. But something looked different –odd, and Karen leaned nearer to examine his head. She gasped and jumped back.

"What's this?" she screamed. "What did you put on my son's forehead?"

Taunt Felice stood up, frightened, and stared at the woman. *Inette* was nowhere to be found.

"What in God's name—? "*Trosclair* broke the tirade as he re-entered the shanty. "Ladee, not again, cahm youself down."

Three children ran in with steaming hot buckets swinging from their little arms. *Trosclair* waved them away. Startled, they ran out. The puppies, however, were in to stay, playing first at *Trosclair's* feet then at Karen's.

"What's this!?" she pointed angrily at Mikie's head.

"Dat," he hesitated "is—is some leever."

"Some **what?**"

"Some leever, some fresh leever. It will hep you boy."

"Liver?! Whose liver, for Christ's sake? And what is it supposed to do? Keep the devil away, too?"

"Look don't holla. Calm youself—"

"No I will not calm myself down! I want—
"Puppies were annoying her at first. Three puppies had scaled her ankles. Curious, she watched them tumble down into a heap. Trosclair held reins on his patience, fixing his gaze on the boy. Karen searched the floor, progressed to the doorway, and looked out. "Where's the spotted one?"

Trosclair peered, trance-like at Mikie. Ultimately, he turned away from the two women and the boy. Puzzled by this gesture, *Taunt Felice* scrutinized his profile, entreating.

Karen felt betrayed by her "mentor;" she groped for the right course of action. She walked back to examine the small organ, almost steaming it as so warm, on his head and covering most of the wound, Revulsion mounted.

"How could they? My God, how could they?" She flared, spinning around to the old lady. "Get this off him!" Without waiting for a response, she shouted to *Trosclair*, "Make her take it off. She listens to you. He shook his head slowly. She countered with "Okay, then I wil-."

Trosclair caught her arm as she reached for Mikie's head and swung her around to face him like a rag doll. "Nahw, you lissen , Ladee. Long yars ago, ah slice ma han real bad on *Gastons'* plow. It don't take no tahm, no, for dat red lahn to crawl up to ma elbow." His eyes, riveted on hers, pushed her head back. She followed them to his finger and watched it trace the imaginary red streak up the inside of his forearm. The same finger pulled her eyes back to his, and he shook it slowly in her face. "Taunt Felice, she save ma lahf de same way she hep you boy nahw. He lowered his face within inches of hers. It was hypnotic. "Dat leever, it suck dat poison out ma han. You see it's well, hunh? It's a good han, yeh? An you know dat it's plenty strong, too. *n'est pas?"* He dropped her attention to regard Mikie.

Karen awoke renewed, her faith restored. She followed *Troclair's* eyes to Mikie, turned to the little boy and squeezed his hand. Chocking back a tear of thanks for his honorable sacrifice, she could hardly look at the boy, feeling shame for her initial reaction. *A small doubt flashed back. I sure hope we're not killing you, honey*. She beat it down.

83

Taunt Felice grinned, relieved, and settled back to her corner and her beads. Trosclair walked to the porch. Karen joined him.

"How can I get to this *Grand*, uh, this town you named?"

"Grand Chanier? We take you, Ladee. You and de boy; we go in de mornin'. We take our pelts to *Grand Chanier* ev'ry Satday. Dey got a telephone. You can call the hospitahl in Lake Charles from dar. You can call Cameron, too. If we har from you fran, we tell him where we take you."

"Just how far is this town? Why couldn't we have done that hours ago?"

"Too far to go to make it in daytahm. Besides, *Taunt Felice*, she know what she doin'." He didn't look at Karen. "An' we would miss suppertahm."

"Supper—well. I don't believe this!" *Trosclair* grinned. "Eatin' tahm is real sarious wit us Cajuns, Ladee. See dose chirren dar?" He pointed to the three diners with their buckets of steam. They decorated the porch steps with yellow hair and greasy mouths. "Dey eatin' crawfish, bahl'd crawfish. *"Tite –Sue, vien ici, Chère."*

The little girl dug deep into her bucket for a warm crawfish, lopping its head off before pulling it from the out. Within seconds, her tiny fingers adeptly cracked and shelled the tail. She popped it into her mouth and started scooping a dark yellow substance from the head with her pinky. She offered it to Karen.

"No, thank you, dear." Karen backed away and returned a weak smile to the little round face.

Trosclair just laughed. He pointed to the center of the village. "You see dat black pot over dar?" Karen knew it well. "It's been cookin' all day long. We kill a *cochon* today."

"A what?" she asked.

"A *cochon*. A pig. We Cajuns don' wast nuttin, cep maybe de squeal." He smiled. "You look green, yeh. But, it's de trute. We eat it ahl. You don' see no buzzard birds round dese parts, do you?" He grinned proudly. She leaned back on the door frame and stared off towards town, *Trosclair* reflected reverently. "And we tank God, too, every day for hepin' to raise our food, or trap our food, and for raisn' our chirren. No, Ladee, we navver eat one ting befor we bow our head and give tanx."

Karen rubbed her ribs, mesmerized by the strange, but pleasant aroma, that filled the night air.

The back of *Trosclair's* head continued to speak to her. "Yes ma'anm we eat it ahl. We making

85

crackling wit de skin, lard wit de fat, cheese wit de head, pickle wit de feet and tail, tripe wit the belly, *citlin* 'and *boudain* wit the gut, *debris* and *bouilllie* wit the organs, and roast de ress on a spit for two days, yeh. Mmm, mmm, *ça c'est bon, oui.* Nahw, he said. if you want to tawk 'bout gumbo, and he turned toward the door smacking his lips---."

But, Karen hadn't wanted to talk about gumbo. Peeking inside he could see her sitting by the bed, her head resting on Mikie's chest. Touched, he quietly shooed the children off the porch steps, and closed the sleeping visitors inside for the night.

Outside, his world came alive with the music of a fiddle and the popping grease. *Trosclair* turned with the chanky-chank of a squeeze box, popped his suspenders and two-stepped off toward town, where his family and friends had already gathered for the night's *fais-do-do*.

The village roused early the following morning, some just to see their visitors off. The pirogues were lined up on the bayou sporting a successful week's trapping. *Trosclair* emerged from his cabin half-dressed, barefoot, wearing a long-john shirt and pants without suspenders. He followed Karen to the river bank, carrying the still unconscious little boy. The sun would be up soon, and the trappers were eager to trade; most were already in the pirogues. Karen stepped ahead of the two boatmen to take her seat. *Trosclair* leaned over to put the boy in her lap. Something fell from his shirt. Karen recognized the small, black, rectangular cloth he had touched to her son's head earlier. *Trosclair* pulled the dark string tied together at the frayed ends up and over his head. He placed it around Mikie's neck. She looked closely at the frayed end, then at the crown of thorns encircling the heart on the cloth at the other end. Karen looked up at *Trosclair* in disbelief. *Trosclair* didn't notice. His eyes remained gently on the boy.

"Dis scapular was giv me bah *Monsignor Droullier* when ah was a boy. It always keep me safe. It will bless you boy, too." he assured her.

"Well," he grinned, "at least it will keep him half safe," he apologized, still grinning. "Ah giv de udder half to a ladee fran long yars ago."

Karen stared back at the big man as he stepped from the boat. "In Burkeville, Texas?" she asked.

Trosclair turned slowly around to face her, his brows knit in surprise,

They just stared at one another for several seconds, each seeing the other for the first time.

"*Trosclair?*" The men awaited his signal. He never broke his gaze. Unsure, he raised his hand, then waved it. Two long poles pushed the little boat from the bank and walked it into the deeper water of the bayou. Karen watched the large man, looking back at her, shrink in the distance. She missed the flutter of Mikie's eyes, her own still frozen on a man, a mere spec at the edge of darkness now fraying into dawn.

Peggy Marceaux

ON A
"WING AND A PRAYER:"
MEMOIR OF A

Third-Generation
Cajun

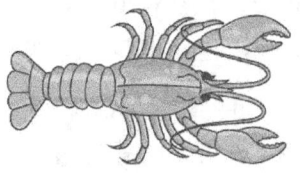

ON A "WING AND A PRAYER:" MEMOIR OF A Third-Generation Cajun

As a third-generation Cajun, raised in Texas, you become quite a perceptive kid. I was born in Louisiana but didn't come across the great Sabine until I was two, so I never was taught Cajun French. I was bored to tears visiting my family over there because that's all they spoke. I managed to grab a few words here and there, but not enough. So, I had to pay close attention to my mom's and dad's reactions. My own parents didn't speak French at home at all unless they were trying to hide something from us kids, so it was quite a guessing game.

Since I was the first born of the first born, I was closer to my mom's sisters and brother and cousins than I was to my own. They started to be born some three or four years after me, and continued for some time. My youngest sister, who is eighteen years younger than I, ~~am~~ is closer to them than I am.

As I was saying, perception became my go-to understanding of what happening with my extended family. For example, one day my mom got a call when I was about twelve. She started talking in French, so I knew it was from relatives in Louisiana. She seemed nonplussed – befuddled. I didn't know what those words meant then, I just knew the feelings. I was listening to Mom's every word, but all I could make out was T-Louis and Helen. T-Louis was my Parin Theo and Nan Nan Lucy's only son from my mother's side of the family, and Helen was his wife. Anyway, I had no idea what had happened, I just understood, in English, we needed to pack our best clothes and go there right away. I couldn't get anything else out of either Mom or Dad all that the way there. They just spoke in French in hushed tones. When we got there, we went to my Taunt Taunt's, who was a sister to Nan Nan Lucy, changed our clothes then went right away to the funeral home in Kaplan. T-Louis was in a casket and Aunt Helen was crying inconsolably. It wasn't until I could talk with Darrell, my cousin, who was 14 and also his nephew, that I found out T-Louis died atop a woman who wasn't his wife. Woohee, but I understood then that Helen's crying became more a wailing **at** him rather than **for** him. I couldn't tell if she wanted to spit in his face or caress it. But things would get hotter when the other woman would show up. That's the only time I've ever seen a fight at a funeral home, hair pulling and all.

The same kind of French got spoken when T-Sue, Mom's double first cousin got pregnant out of wedlock. I was kept in the dark until it started showing on her. She never married. The same thing happened to her mom, Taunt Taunt. That's how she got her older brother Michael. But my Grandma got her brother Eddie, to marry Taunt Taunt. And, that's how we got T-Sue. That made her moms double first cousin. What a family I had.

And the same type of French speaking happened when Uncle Isaac and Aunt Helen (a different Helen) had an affair. Yes, they were married to other people. There was a rumor circling that Aunt Helen would open the window to her bedroom and let Uncle Isaac in while her husband was asleep-absolutely shameful.

Otherwise, I always enjoyed going to Nan Lucy's, except for one time when Parin told something to Darrell in French I didn't understand, but there was nothing new in that. He left his grandfather's and went into a shed. He said he'd be out in a minute, so I didn't follow him in. He came out with a paper bag, and I didn't say anything about it, until he was about to throw it into a big canal by their house.

"What's in the bag?" I asked.

"Oh, some little *chiens*." he answered after he had already hauled back and thrown the bag.

92

"What are *chiens*?" I asked

"Some new-born puppies," he answered as the bag was already flying through the air.

"NO!" I screamed.

"Oh," he said, "Ah didn't tink to ax chu if chu wanted dem."

"Darrell! Why are you drowning new-born puppies?" I cried.

"Well, de feed costs money."

"You need to lop the balls off the males, or get the females spayed. Don't take it out on the puppies!" I was horrified.

He said tell my Grandpa. I did, but he just laughed at me. Grrrrr. My ignorant, inhumane, relatives!

Normally, we had fun, though, like the times we played football, but what happened to those puppies put me in a bad mood for the rest of the day. The next day was as a better one. But, once, when Darrell got hot, he wanted to go to the Dairy, so I followed him there. He opened the lid on a vat of fresh, homogenized milk that they had gotten from their cows that morning. He took a dipper and got him a slurp of some cool milk, and then handed me the dipper to get me some. I passed. Who knows who'd be getting the bottles of milk from those vats that day? Or any day for that matter? Something tells me that's not the first time that's happened.

We'd often go inside the fence of the beef cattle Parin had and throw dried patties at one another. We tried hard not to get shocked by the pulsing wires that held in the cattle. But, once, when I was climbing out, my hair got caught on one of the barbs. My brain felt every pulsing shock of the wire. I couldn't get loose, so like any frustrated twelve-year-old, I got scared and started to cry. Darrell ran to the house and got my mom, who came running out with a pair of scissors (I know, you shouldn't run with scissors, but I was glad that time she did). Parin came out, too, and went straight for the breaker box, which I appreciated. Mom cut my hair first, and I went into the house to lie down. I could still feel the pulsing wire in my head.

Usually, I loved being in the house when the women were first preparing the meal. When it was seafood gumbo, which was my favorite, I'd be standing by the stove while they were cooking the rice, always on a gas stove. Invariably they'd burn the bottom of the rice in the pot because they liked their rice very dry. They'd give us kids the burned rice part and call it *graton*; they said it was a kind of crispy, poor-man's candy. The other women cut up the Trinity: bell pepper, onion and celery, while Nan Nan would make the roux. She used 1/2 cup of lard, with a 1 tsp. of sugar that would turn to syrup over medium to high heat; when the oil was ready for the flour. When it was, she would sift in 1/2-3/4 cup of flour into it. That's when the work would start, because she would have to stir it non-stop until the roux was the color of an old penny.

Then, when it was that color, she would pour a gallon of water in the pot, put the onions in and boil it for approximately one to two hours. After that, she'd add the rest of the Trinity and crab and let simmer for 30 minutes. She'd add the oysters, shrimp, green onions and parsley the last fifteen minutes. No filé for this family, thank you.

Or, since it was Easter, she may opt for crawfish *étoufée*. Yum. Darrell and I would just go to the rice field that had already gone to seed and get a burlap bag of how ever many crawfish Nan Nan wanted. Usually that was however many people she was cooking for. Let's say it was for four, just to give us a baseline; she would increase it from there. We'd have to boil the crawfish before she could use them because we'd have to peel the tails and extract the fat from the heads. For four, she'd need 2 lbs of peeled crawfish tails, 1/4 cup of oil, ½ up of chopped celery, 1 cup of chopped onions, ½ cup of chopped bell pepper, 2 TBS of crawfish fat, 2 cups of cold water, 2 tsps corn starch and 1/4 cup chopped onion tops (green onions) and parsley.

She'd season the crawfish tails with salt, black pepper, and cayenne pepper or Tony Chachere and set them aside. Then, she'd add the Trinity to a heavy pot and cook until onions were wilted, stirring constantly. She'd add 1½ cups of water, crawfish fat and crawfish tails, bring it to a boil, then cover over low heat for 30 mins, stirring constantly. Finally, she'd dissolve the corn starch into ½ cup of water and add it to mixture. The onion tops and parsley, would go in the last ten minutes and be served over cooked rice.

Or, she may decide on a shrimp *creole*. Here, again, this is based on four people. She would need the same thing: the Trinity, but here a red bell pepper, for color only, cherry tomatoes cut in half, and coconut creamer to balance the acidity. Since she didn't need to boil the shrimp first, she could boil it for stock. If it doesn't make enough stock, she could add vegetable stock to it. Afterward, she would peel the shrimp and boil the shells for stock. Same with all, but she'd use tomatoes and she'd have used olive oil for health reasons. She'd add tomatoes and shrimp at the very last, season it all with a little cayenne pepper and Emerile's Essence, and serve it over rice.

Or, she could make a *coubion*, or poached fish. She'd put 1 inch of water in her pan, 2 cloves of garlic, 40 peppercorns, a bay leaf, some parsley flakes, ½ cup of dry wine or sherry then bring it to a boil, simmer, and bring to a boil again. Then she'd drop a red fish or a snapper in the mixture and simmer for five minutes. If not tender enough, she'd bake it until the meat was very tender, and serve it over rice.

Then another time, again, when I was twelve or thirteen, Taunt Taunt's house was right in the pathway of a tornado. Her family and some friends were playing *bourré* one night when they were having bad weather. Suddenly, they heard a loud train coming. The tornado lifted the house, turned it completely around and laid it back down on its foundation. My folks didn't speak French to them on the phone; there was no reason to. When T-Sue's baby was born, she named her Josette and asked me to be her Godmother. I accepted it with all the responsibilities that came along with it, because I was a devote Catholic back then. I stayed true to those vows until she married. I also bought her a tee shirt everywhere I went, which covered a lot of ground because I was an avid angler in New Mexico, Arkansas and Colorado. It was just a reminder that I was thinking of her.

Taunt Taunt and her husband Eddie used to grow the sweetest little butter beans. She would always cook them for me with sugar on them, and put them on top of rice. Oh, they were so good. I remember her for them and for her pickled eggs. They were to die for! I always left her house wanting to go back. She'd soak her eggs in a kind of pickled juice that was mostly sweet. Sometimes I try to replicate them, but I can't. What I'd give to go back for just once and get the recipe now that I'm older.

I can remember going to my Dad's true brother's once. He had a passel of step brothers and sisters, though, when I got older, I was informed that his stepfather, Rudoph Lege, never married his mother. Anyway, he had one blood older brother named Lion, and one blood older sister, named Verna. Verna was a head case, and I truly do mean that. She used to hide under the table when she had company. Or, she'd be locked in a room. She had one son I liked, and owed my life to, because, when I was just ten, my little brother, Chuck got swept away in the current of the river, and I went after him. Don't know what I could have done because I couldn't swim either. Gabie, Verna's son, swam after us and hauled us both in. I've been indebted to him and kept up with him the rest of my life. He had an older sister named Cathy. He showed me a picture of her in the nursing home; it was terrible. They had her tied to a chair. Obviously, she ended up like her mother. I felt so sorry for both her and his family, though my family didn't escape the "curse." either. My sister, Gail, the sibling right after me was a very good journalist. She wrote for the Port Arthur and Beaumont News, then went west and ran the Pueblo newspaper. But, as it does with girls, she was ambushed by Schizophrenia after she turned 25. It hit her hard. She had been talking to imaginary people all her life, though, so I wasn't surprised. I had to go get her in Santa Barbara. She tried to throw her head out the window all the way home, and that's with the windows up and the doors locked. She talked gibberish incessantly. Only once did I cry, though. That was when she was lying down on the couch having sex with a phantom lover. I had to get my Grandmother out to the house to sit with her while I went to work. Nothing like that had hit any other one of us in that time, so this took us totally unawares. I checked her into a psychiatric hospital and went home to my own issues that were starting to materialize: mood swings, anger issues, rages, depression, etc. I sought out a psychiatrist myself. My little brother, Chuck, started with paranoia and rages himself. But, he was in the Air Force, so they were seeing him in there. My younger brother, Greg, didn't have any of those problems, and I was glad. He was just a stickler for being on time like my dad, but all of us were, so I didn't see a problem in that. My baby sister had a few anger issues, but when she found the right husband all of those seem to have gone away. My dad, however, could be mean and suffered from depression. He self-medicated by drinking-*a lot*. He would never see a doctor, and died of a coronary occlusion at 47.

There's been lots of miles and time since then. My Taunt Taunt's son, Michael, married a girl from up north and moved to Ohio. His wife had died by this time and he been in a nursing home. My Taunt Taunt died of stomach cancer. Of course, whoever among all of us who was living and well enough made the journey across the Sabine to the funeral. For example, when my dad died   so young, that brought all of his family as well as ours that were still living over there here for it. I say here, because much of my mom's family came to Texas with us. Dad had convinced most of them to come over because he learned carpentry skills over here, and knew they could, too. So, Grandpa, Roland, my Aunt Pat's husband, Lolan, my Aunt Jane's husband, and Gerald, Mom's brother came, too. That took care of my mom's family. My Aunt Debbie hadn't been born, yet, and Gerald was still in high school. For some strange reason, my Dad wasn't as close to his family as he was to my mom's. Anyway, I'm getting ahead of myself. Before T-Sue had Josette, her dad, Eddie died of a heart attack. We all went to his funeral. After T-Sue had Josette, she grew up and married Wayne Duhan. After Taunt Taunt died, and we went to that funeral, Wayne built T-Sue a metal home on their property right next to their home. Josette's two girls married; one lived on their property and one moved to Baton Rouge. T-Louis and Helen had a son, Dale who married Brenda, a member of Dad's family, and I've lost track of the other kids he had. Sis had Nell Dean, Millie and Joey. Grace had Darrell, Donnie and Leta. I've lost track of their kids. Of course, Parin died sometime earlier, then Nan Nan Lucy, and we went to their funerals. It seemed like that was the only times we got together. Then, my grandma died, and Mom in 2002 they said from Pancreatic Cancer. But I don't believe that because she was in pain. Anyway, I think very few came, but I was all strung out emotionally, so don't quote me on that. Then when my sister, Gail, died, in 2004, I know nobody came from Louisiana. It was a shock to us all, and I'm ashamed to say, a relief.

My dad had five half-siblings: Rudy, Pearl, Gilbert, Eugene and Eva. Eugene is the only one who made anything out of himself, getting a PhD in social work, and getting a good job in Houston in social work.

When my dad started drinking, when I knew him at least, his beer of choice was Pearl. Then, for some reason, it became Schlitz. He drank that until the evening before he died. Dad passed on his love for tobacco and alcohol to the three of his kids that were more susceptible to it. That would be me, Chuck and Greg. Because I started having major lung problems when I left college, I wouldn't chance the tobacco, but Chuck and Greg did. I did, however imbibe in alcohol, and like Chuck, and later, Greg, quite heavily at times. All that had to stop when Chuck and I were put on meds. When Shelly came along, I didn't keep up with her. I know she drank, but I never knew how much. I enjoyed hard liquor much sooner than beer. In fact, that and my life's choices took me to the threshold of suicide, though I did not cross it, because, obviously I'm writing this. Still, it was enough to alarm all of my friends and family. I also had mental problems that I had inherited from my Dad, particularly rages, anger issues and depression. My brother, Greg, asked me to go into an upscale mental facility in Cincinnati, which I agreed to do. It probably saved my life. I did two stints in that hospital, the first one was for a month, the last one, two weeks for depression. Chuck did something similar in the Service. He came out clean from alcohol, and his mental problems were under control for the time being. Greg never suffered from mental problems, and neither did, Shelly, the youngest of us all. I'm so glad. It's a curse, a real curse; I can't tell you what Gail put us through. My mother and her new husband abdicated all responsibilities for Gail. That was an exceptional hardship to those of us just beginning our lives and trying to hold down jobs. Really, Chuck never did a thing to help out in that cause, or any cause for that matter. He was dealing with his own problems. Greg, Shelly and I shouldered all the monetary responsibilities for Mom, from getting her hearing aids, to helping with her teeth problems, to purchasing her a new used car, to getting her out of bankruptcy. From the time she last went into the hospital, Mom was dead in two days.

Unfortunately, as with most curses, it lives on in our genes. Though Shelly didn't display any signs herself, she has a child who did, as did, Chuck, and Greg, who each has a child who presented with a myriad of mental problems. All of my siblings are doing their best to live with the disabilities, because they are, after all, life-long responsibilities. I feel sorry for them and am so glad that I didn't contribute to the family curse, and that I talked my sister, Gail, again and again, out of having children. I tried to help out when I could; for Shel, that turned out to be more of a problem than a help, for which I am sorry. For Chuck and his wife Deb, I think it has been more of a help, and I'm glad. They have a fine son. The problem has come primarily from some of my dad's relatives marrying first cousins, from the time when generations up the family tree, my great, great, great, great uncle's, whose death is depicted on the *arc de triumph,* nephew, Francois Marceau, brought his first cousin, Azelie Stelly, on the boat with him, to marry in America. It started there; then, again, just two generation after that, my great, great uncle Araste Marceaux married his first cousin. Leomire Marceaux. So, the die was set. I think even before them, Cleo Marceaux and Margarete Touchet were somehow related, as well. Then, on his mother's side, four generations up, Clet LeBanc married Aurelia LeBlanc, and two generations later, Adam LeBlanc married Even Maria LeBlanc. Dad's maternal family was rife with first cousins marrying. It's no wonder we aren't all in the looney bin.

So, life goes on. Chuck's now a retired minister, Greg is a successful employee in the recycling business who is pretty high up the chain of command. He loves his job. He helps his kids a lot of the time with financial woes. He also loves to golf, and keeps up with the tournaments with me by texting what's going on blow by blow, especially by supporting our favorite players. Shelly works for the judicial system with computers as a systems analysis. She's looking forward to retirement. She has quite a few physical ailments, especially for her age. But, she's always a trooper, never complains and works harder at making her grandkids and her family have a good time and eat well than anyone I know. As a third-generation Cajun she does her part in making gumbo and potato salad. She and her family love crawfish and *boudin* balls as much as I do.

Now, I just spend my time at home and going to physical therapy for my balance. I fall a lot. I can't get out and walk with my walker on my long driveway, which I'd love to do, because it's 106 out there as I'm writing this, so I just write on my computer so much I've developed carpal tunnel in my left wrist. But, as my friend, Mike, who also has Parkinson's, told me, you can't let it define you, so I'm not. But I can't get out and play golf anymore like he can. If I'd try to swing a club, I'd fall over. I feel like mine is progressing a little faster than his is, because of the amount of exercise he can get that I can't. So, I write stories. And, I have a lot to write about. When I was young, I was a good athlete, and I loved to move and play sports. I played volleyball through college and also helped my team win State in '68. As I got older, I wasn't happy unless I could be playing softball, tennis, racket ball, or golf. My 40-acre ranch in Sequin helped me transfer sport into caring for cattle, horses, chickens and seeing to the hay field. I was outside and in my element. Then, in 2012, we sold the ranch, it was all downhill for me since then. In 2014 my inherited arthritic spine needed to have four lumbar vertebrae fused and a synovial cyst removed. That was quite an ordeal to get over; that followed with a cervical fusion of two vertebrae in 2016. In 2019 I was diagnosed with Parkinson's and in 2021 had a Deep Brain Stimulator implanted in my head to control the tremors. I also have lung problems as I referred to earlier. My dad smoked three packs of cigarettes a day and night. He'd often wake up at night and smoke and think about how much lumber he needed to order for his next job. He smoked in the house, outside, in the car, wherever. My mom ended up with COPD and I ended up with Bronchectisis, a type of COPD that does not respond to oxygen. I have a Hill Rom Vita Cough, a Hill Rom Vest attached by hoses to an Airway Clearance Machine and nebulizer that goes with it. So, I have plenty to do in the house besides write. If I don't use these machines, I develop an inordinate amount of mucous in my lungs that begs to come out. Heck, I've already had fourteen surgeries in my life. Now, I'm sure other third-generation Cajuns have suffered the same consequences, since almost all had dads and moms smoked back then. Another consequence we're seeing is the result of the refineries in the Beaumont-Port Arthur area expelling their gases. We've had babies born with twelve fingers. The doctors ask the parents if they are from the Golden Triangle: bad thing to be asked.

As far as my education goes, from the time I was young, I've always gotten by on a "wing and a prayer." I had this athletic sense about me that was intuitive and far superior to my academic abilities and interests, so my athletic abilities and interests were always foremost in my mind. Always. My interests in my body moving started far earlier than my elementary years. I was always outdoors, when the weather and my parents allowed me, doing whatever. As much as I love cats today, once I wrapped a tea towel around one, turned round and round and slung her like I would have a sling-shot stone. Oh, she landed fine and, on her feet, but today that bothers me just a little. And I captured a dragon fly and bound her up by the wings with rubber bands in my mom's washing shed for a day or so before I let her go. That, and I played with old mice bones in Dad's garage where he stored all his roofing shingles. I got a tape worm doing it, so God was good to help me get rid of it. Finally, I received a glove, bat and ball for Christmas, so all the C's I got from my nuns at St. Mary's Elementary School for deportment went away. That changed my life for the better. That, and I had a brother born eleven months after my sister, Gail, who was such a girly girl and was too interested in reading books and talking to the characters in her head to play catch with me. In middle school at St. Elizabeth's my interests in softball exploded, and my academic career decreased to more B's than A's. We actually had a TEAM. Wow! I found that I could hit the ball farther than, and could throw the ball more accurately, and faster than anyone, so I was moved to defend third base, then short stop. We also started playing volleyball at recess. I found I was good at that, too. While in high school they, sadly, didn't have a softball team, but they did a volleyball team, and we had a softball league that formed up outside of school. So, I got the best of both worlds. I played for the Cardinals in the outside league and Port Neches-Groves in school. My academic grades improved, too, because my dad held reins over me there. He also was a stickler for picking out what classes I should take, because he just knew I was going to go to a two-year business college, and wanted me to get in all the businesses classes I could to prepare. I knew I wanted to go to a four-year college, so all the electives I took were academic courses. He made me take two years of typing, two years of shorthand, one year of bookkeeping and I don't remember what else. I took two years of anatomy, one year of chemistry and one year of physics, my only C. Of course, I took English every year, and honors English my junior and senior years. I was so eaten up with athletics I finally told him I was going to go to a four-year college if I had to move out and work to pay for it myself. That's when my Mom was pregnant for my little sister, Shelly. He decided I might be of more help staying there and helping Mom with the baby, so he relented and made me an offer: if I'd live there and help her out, he'd pay for my tuition only.

Books weren't cheap then, but I'd see what I could do about them, so I agreed to the deal. That allowed me to play for the Lamar Volleyball Team, and I'm glad, because we won State in 1968. I couldn't believe they didn't have a softball team, but they didn't back then. They had a basketball team, but I had never played basketball, so I turned them down for that sport. I majored in English because that was my strongest academic class in high school, but I came up woefully short in achievement. I made nothing but B's at Lamar. Part of it was that I could not find a book I could borrow; I surely couldn't buy them. I attended a class where I needed seven paperback books for the entire class. I was all ears at lecture time because I couldn't afford to buy any of them. So, I made a B in that class, too, on a "wing and a prayer." Little was I to know it was just the beginning of my "wing and a prayers."

A few years later, when I was hired on at Alvin High to teach English, my Department Chair approached me to start a Gifted and Talented Class. I eagerly agreed. That meant I could develop my own curriculum, since there hadn't been such a class before. We read Charles Dickens and I put forth the idea that we develop stationery to sell at Dickens on the Strand in Galveston, using Pip, Estella, Ms. Haversham and Magwitch as the stationery, and house it in a cart like they used to sell things in Dickens' time. They liked the idea, so I checked with teachers in the building trades department, the speech, department, the art department and the drama department. They all agreed to take part in tutoring my students. So, I asked for volunteers for building the cart, volunteers for drawing and painting the stationery then binding it in string, volunteers for learning the British cockney dialect and volunteers for selecting the costumes. We had a great time doing that. The only deadline we had was when Dickens on the Strand would take place. My job was to get the okay from my Department Chair, the permit for

Dickens on the Strand, the transportation for the students and the cart and the types of lanterns they required we have. All turned out well and we had a ball. I think that won me points with my Department Chair, though that's not why I did it. That, as well as in taking part in the Ambassador's People to People Program that Alvin was invited to that summer. We were allowed to take so many juniors and seniors and had to have a sponsor. We would be having one week of home stay-overs in Ireland, England, the Netherlands and France, a month in all. I was so excited to get to go because I had just learned my great uncle's seven times removed, funeral was depicted in a frieze on the *Arc de Triomphe* facing the *Champs Élyées*. The trip was not only the best learning experience for teaching British lit, but it was the best trip of my life. That influenced my Department Chair to give me a shot at being Department Chair when she left to become principal. She gave the Chair to a woman I truly admire to this day, because she was so worthy of it. She was a wonderful, and very knowledgeable teacher compared to me. I was just a third-generation Cajun pulling myself up by my bootstraps and getting by on a "wing and a prayer," after all, learning right along with my students. To better prepare myself, I started on my Master' Degree at UHCLC. I had a conversation with my advisor at the college who was very concerned with my vocabulary. I promised her I would improve, and to this day I have kept that promise. She asked if I thought I was ready to teach British Lit? I told her by the time I got this degree it would take me a long way there. She said she was concerned, and asked if there were other teachers there who would deserve the job first? I said yes, but in my opinion, with my experiences and ambition, I thought I was the best they could get. So, I set about earning that opinion, taking the classes I would need, and improving my vocabulary; but, the "wing and a prayer," had branded me for life. There's a part of me that I can't shake: the fact that I came from an ignorant culture that didn't encourage its kids to read books. Anyway, once that Chair retired, I was selected for Chair over everybody else. Good English teachers resented me. I didn't blame them.

I worked hard at going to workshops that would help me teach teachers how to improve student composition, and I learned new vocabulary right along with the students. My tests would be one-page compositions that were related to what we were studying where they would have to plug the proper spelling of the vocabulary word in it. They looked forward to the unit or book we were studying, especially when it was it was relatable to their lives, and I made sure they were.

I was pretty good about myself, until I moved to my 40-acre ranch in Seguin and started teaching at Smithson Valley High. I was treated with distain because they had a tight-nit English Department that wasn't at all receptive to a new teacher, especially one who had been

Department Chair. That intimidated the Department Chair something fierce. Fortunately for me, I retired in 2002, ostensibly to help my little sister take care of my mom, but she died in January of that year. I don't miss that school, one bit, just the friends I made there, and I missed what my students and I had managed to accomplish. I had invited the Ruseryrra boys to come speak to us after their escaping the genocide in Burundi with their dad and making it to Botswana. Their names were John, Vanalet and Paul, ten, nine and eight respectively, that was quite an education. They came back to New Braunfels with our then ambassador, Bob Krueger. I have a picture of the boys below; they were an eye-opener to my students. I loved them having the experience.

Plus, I have a letter I wrote to the Education Agency with my students asking for an alternative curriculum for potential drop outs or students not as interested in "sit-down" classes. I also have the letter they wrote to us in reply.

John   Jamalet   Mark
10   9   11

Below I have copied a page of my syllabus and the novels we both read as a class and were required to read.

At this time, August of 2023, I am 74 years old, but will be 75 in December; both my brothers were born in June. They are 4 ½ and 9 years younger than I am respectively, so that makes Chuck 70 and Greg 65. Chuck is looking forward to getting to see his granddaughter more often; Greg is looking forward to Medicare; Shelly is 18 years younger, so she just had a birthday this month. She is 57 and looking forward to retirement.

What has time done to my little brothers and sister? What has time done to me? Since I've already bought my plot and headstone, I guess I'm looking forward to my long dirt nap. I won't mind it. I need rest, both mentally and physically. I've already done what I need to do, anyway. I wrote a series of children's books about chickens called *BeakSpeak,* in honor of my Seguin chickens, and three more collections of adult short stories, so far, including this one, the Cajun series. So, if it weren't for the animals and people I've hurt, I'm pretty pleased with my life.

English I Agenda for April 3 – 7 <small>Marceaux</small>

Monday: Pre-AP—fiction writing: discuss hooks, -ing verbs with helper verbs, and reteach correct dialogue format with flesh outs; only one rough draft reading before final due date: B day is April 7th; A day is April 10th; need poetry devices sheet: introduce imagistic poetry and tropes (Ezra Pound and Alice Walker poems): analyze Rod McKuen's excerpt from "Information" and its tropish rewrite; a published, tropeless poem or excerpt with your tropish rewrite due b.o.p. next class meeting

R—conclude alternate ending script to *Of Mice and Men* project; individual and group contribution, props, and artwork finalized; begin rehearsal and practice filming next class meeting; first set (barn) in classroom – second set (novel's opening and ending scene) outside in trees behind teacher's A-wing parking lot; return vocab. pckt. 4 and go over for quiz on Friday, the 7th

Tuesday: Pre-AP, R—see Monday

Wednesday: Pre-AP—tropeless poem and rewrite due in tray b.o.p.; hand out song / lyrics assignment sheet requirements; group into 3's; must commit to song by next class meeting; sign up to present (beginning the week of April 10th) today: will present one song with lyrics a day, 10 mins. max (if one or two partners is/are absent on that day, you must present anyway; partner(s) absent will need to submit a different song second class meeting after absence

R—props, costumes, backdrop due b.o.p.; hand out copies of scripts to actors & directors: begin 1 of 3-day rehearsals (all actors must have lines memorized by 3rd rehearsal day—**there will be no under studies, so actors must not be absent!**); begin practice filming at "barn" set: DAILY GRADES WILL BE TAKEN ON YOUR PARTICIPATION AND CONTRIBUTIONS TO THAT DAY'S ACTIVITIES AND SUCCESS

Thursday: Pre-AP, R—see Tuesday

Friday: Pre-AP—introduce Rogerian Argument for informed (researched), collaborative paper: the project will culminate in a class debate; hand out the format and example outline; go over "problem" (introductory) paragraph; choose partner / opponent then formulate problem and compose problem paragraph together: due e.o.p.

R—vocab. quiz 4; need scripts, props, etc., for Day 2 rehearsals and filming

AP III: Masterworks Addendum
Cultural Diversity in Novels

During the 1st semester, it is a requirement that you read one of the novels below for one of your masterworks. I encourage you to read others on your own, and we will be doing the designated novels as a class. I may add to this list later.

A Summer Place, Gary Soto
Nectar in a Sieve, Markandaza
House of Spirits, Allende (any of her books)
Nisei Daughter, Sone
Sound of Waves, Mishima
House on Mango Street, Cisneros
Hunger of Memory, Rodriquez
Clover, Dorrie Saunders
Woman Warrior, Kingston
Canyons, Paulsen
Floating World, Kadohata
Learning to Bow, Feller
No Longer at Ease, Achebe
The Chosen, Chaim Potok
Animal Dreams, Kingsolver

Class novels (don't use for individual masterworks):

  Bless Me Ultima, Anaya
* Gathering of Old Man, Gaines
* Yellow Raft in a Blue Water, Dorris
* Snow Falling on Cedars, Guterson
* The Bean Trees, Kingsolver
  Beloved, Morrison

English IV Syllabus 1998 Semester I <small>Marceaux</small>

Time frame:	2000 B.C. - 1600 A.D.
Prehistory reference:	Neolithic Stonehenge
Language:	Old, Middle, and Early Modern English History of English Etymology Language chart
Vocabulary:	Packets 1 - 6, SAT analogies, literature-generated
Cultural heritage:	Celtic Anglo-Saxon Viking French
Religion:	Norse mythology Roman Catholic Anglican
Monarchs:	Alfred the Great William the Conqueror Edward the Confessor War of the Roses The Tudors The Stewarts
Literature:	A-S riddles Viking epic *Beowulf* Chaucer's *The Canterbury Tales* Shakespeare's *Macbeth*
Videos:	*Stonehenge* *History of the Language* *Erik the Viking* *Braveheart* (opt.) *William Wallace* (opt.) *Lady Jane* *Macbeth*
Resources:	*Heath English Level 12* *English Tradition* Related videos, maps, and notes

Scope and Sequence English IV Advanced Placement

Course focus   on critical thinking, reading, and writing skills that will facilitate timed literary analysis and multiple choice practice testing over multi-genre literature; a cross section of novels selected from the College Board Masterlist.; and a study in world literature, cross-gender and multicultural perspectives. Literary terms and vocabulary work are ongoing.

<u>1st Semester</u>:   *focus* on dynamics of gender roles and power of myth

1st 6 wks.:	review timed writing and test taking strategies	1/2 wk.
	Joseph Campbell's *The Power of Myth: Hero of a Thousand Faces*	
	Chinua Achebe's *Things Fall Apart*	2 wks.
	Shadow of the Wolf	1/2 wk.
	practice timed writings and multiple choice tests	2 wks.
	writing responses to the works studied: focus on commonalities among cultures	1/2 wk.
2nd 6 wks.:	Amy Tan's *The Joy Luck Club*	2 1/2 wks.
	Anglo-Saxon era and *Beowulf*	1 1/2 wks.
	practice timed writing and multiple choice tests	2 wks.
3rd 6 wks.:	the middle ages and Geoffrey Chaucer's *The Canterbury Tales*: *Wife of Bath's Prologue and Tale* or the *Nun's Priest's Tale*	2 wks.
	Renaissance: *Elizabeth Rex*: her final days	1/2 wk.
	Shakespeare's *Hamlet*, *Othello*, or *King Lear* and *The Taming of the Shrew*	3 wks.
	practice timed writing and multiple choice tests	1/2 wk.

Peggy Marceaux

Jim Nelson
Commissioner of Education
Texas Education Agency
1701 N. Congress Ave.
Austin, Texas 78701-1494

Dear Commissioner Nelson:

Ms. Marceaux's freshman regular English class members of Smithson Valley High School would like for you to consider a voluntary nautical experience on the Gulf of Mexico as an alternative to Texas' traditional alternative schools and courses created for would-be drop outs and behavioral problems. For years, Texas has invested time and money in class rooms, teachers, and computers that offer, at best, an artificial life experience to troubled teens. After reading an excerpt from Junger's *The Perfect Storm*, and Longfellow's "The Wreck of the Hesperus," then viewing the video *White Squall*, all based on true stories, we discovered that real-life challenges at sea can teach important life skills and build strong characters in a matter of mere weeks.

We learned the sea can teach you skills such as discipline, respect, and responsibility. You need discipline to get up each chilly morning before sunrise and perform crucial tasks that might decide, for instance, whether a sail is tied securely enough to withstand an unexpected gust of wind. Mr. Moore from *The Perfect Storm* needs discipline to concentrate on the steps it takes for him to successfully rescue the Satori crew in the middle of that life-threatening hurricane. Another important skill is learning how to respect yourself as well as other crew members. Respect leads to valuing others' opinions, compromising, and contributing to a team effort. In *White Squall*, for instance, Preston doesn't respect himself enough *not* to cheat on tests. Members of his crew, however, show him that they have faith in his abilities by tutoring him, which enables him to pass his finals and stay on the ship. A final skill, responsibility, is probably the most important skill a sailor can acquire at sea, the greatest of which falls on the captain's shoulders. If a captain does not appreciate the power of the sea, and therefore jeopardizes his crew, the results could be tragic, as it was for the captain of The Hesperus in Longfellow's poem. He was certain he could safely navigate through yet another hurricane, but that final image of the captain's small daughter, washed up on shore while still tied to the broken mast, will haunt readers forever. In addition to life skills, many quality character traits learned aboard a vessel are essential in every day life.

We learned that the sea will also quickly draw out courage, leadership traits, and humility. Courage is often hard to muster, but the sea will bring it out in you in an instant. When the helicopter drops Mr. Moore into the huge swells of that "Perfect Storm," the rescuer puts his safety last. He focuses every ounce of his energy and concern on getting the two women and Captain Leonard into wet suits and then the rescue basket. He completely forgets about himself until he is safely seated in the helicopter again. Likewise, our class members found facing such adversity hones the toughest rebels into rock-solid leaders. Such is Skipper Sheldon of *White Squall*. His previous experience with the sea's challenges enables him to demonstrate a more genuine wisdom and honesty than even the sacred American courtroom. Finally, we learned that the sea is a powerful ego-crusher, and that Mother Nature must be respected each and every moment of each and every voyage. Experience is a great teacher, but even though Skipper Sheldon had experienced a number of ocean storms, he "trips" on a white squall, something he'd never been through before. Likewise, the captain of The Hesperus mistakes that last hurricane for all the previous ones he'd negotiated successfully. As a result, everyone on board died. He simply forgets he is merely a man. Humility would have saved him, his crew, and his little girl.

These same skills and character traits can develop at sea without facing life-threatening situations. What matters here is it's real life, in close quarters, with everyone depending on everyone else, and it takes less time than traditional alternative schools. Since Texas doesn't yet have a 0 % drop-out rate, why not try something new? As long as the state enrolls students on a voluntary basis, it has much more to gain than to lose.

English I Regular, 5th period class

TEXAS EDUCATION AGENCY

1701 North Congress Ave ★ Austin, Texas 78701-1494 ★ 512/463-9734 ★ FAX: 512/463-9838 ★ http://www.tea.state.tx.us

Jim Nelson
Commissioner of Education

October 27, 2000

Ms. Peggy Marceaux, English Department Chair
Comal Independent School District
Smithson Valley High School
14001 Highway 46 West
Spring Branch, Texas 78070

Dear Ms. Marceaux and Students of the English I Regular, 5th Period Class:

Thank you for your recent letter requesting that I consider a voluntary nautical experience on the Gulf of Mexico as an alternative to Texas' traditional alternative schools and courses for would-be dropouts and students with behavioral problems. I admire the depth of research and teamwork demonstrated in producing your letter. You articulately expressed your thoughts concerning opportunities for growth and learning provided by nautical experiences. Clearly, your classroom has afforded you a safe port to read, view, discuss, and reflect on the actions of others as they ventured against the sea and its unbridled fury.

Character is developed experientially over a period of time as a result of an infinite number of challenges and experiences. The same skills that make a person successful in one environment are transferable to many different environments. Some of our daily challenges may not be as glamorous or exciting as those from the sea, but they are every bit as daunting and, more importantly, we draw from those experiences at the times that we are challenged to the depths of our inner core. Therefore, I urge you to look for the challenges and opportunities for character development and skill building in your daily lives, even if your daily experiences do not bring you face to face with twenty-foot swells and one hundred mile-an-hour winds.

You make an interesting case for experiential learning; however, I am not in a position to "approve" or "disapprove" your request. Decisions regarding the specific location at which a school district chooses to provide instruction in the curriculum required by the Texas Education Code and State Board of Education rules are ultimately the responsibility of the board of trustees of the district. Thus, your request is more appropriately addressed to your local school board. State law, however, does require students to be in attendance with a teacher to be counted for funding purposes. Whether your proposal would entitle the school district to funding is something I cannot answer without knowing the arrangements for teachers and curriculum.

Thank you for your energy, enthusiasm, and interest in bringing this proposal to my attention. I wish each of you the very best in your educational and personal endeavors.

Sincerely,

Jim Nelson
Commissioner of Education

Preparing Children, Promoting Excellence

ABOUT THE AUTHOR
PEGGY MARCEAUX

Peggy Marceaux is a retired English teacher who lives in Canyon Lake, Texas. She earned her Bachelor's Degree from Lamar University and her Masters of Arts from the University of Houston, where she specialized in British Literature.

Ms. Marceaux taught for 32 years; 11 in the Alvin Independent School District and 15 in the Comal Independent School District in TX, Chairing the High School English Departments in both.

Having raised chickens for twenty years, she loved the diversity among the breeds. This inspired "BeakSpeak", a story designed to help young people accept their differences and build confidence, through speech validation. Ever the English teacher, Ms. Marceaux believes the earlier you teach children language precision, the better it will help them succeed in their future relationships and careers.

Along with BeakSpeak, Ms. Marceaux is also involved with CLAW the Canyon Lake Area Writers at the Tye Preston Memorial Library in Canyon Lake, Texas where they meet for two hours the first and third Tuesday of each month. They enjoy letting their creative juices flow with writing prompts, have visiting speakers import helpful knowledge, and submit their 5,000-to-8,000-word short stories to Raconteur in the hopes of gaining publicity.

Short Story Collections:

About BeakSpeak – the Characters

The BeakSpeak characters are inspired from Peggy's own chickens! Some 30+ years ago Peggy began raising chickens on her farm and discovered that chickens have personalities. Along with their very personable characteristics they must learn quickly that there is a pecking order. Like human society, some chickens behave aggressively, others passively, and weak birds cannot survive a bully without a human intervening.

Her chicken coop, then became the English classroom, where Ms. Marceaux taught language skills for 32 years in high school. "My greatest reward was watching my students grow to respect one another, find their confidence, learn how to rationally think about the world around them, and then shape their views to fit in that world. I was able to help them do all this by teaching them that, when you think, speak and write precisely and concisely, using the clearest and most effective words, with the most energetic verbs to defend your views, the better you communicate your meaning."

The first BeakSpeak book is a colorful rendition of a classroom of chickens who are learning about thinking and language skills. Add to those techniques, Marceaux stimulates thought with her exploratory questions, and suggested answers. BeakSpeak, A Fable and Language Workbook is a perfect companion piece with this book as everyone can benefit from learning how to better communicate with others!

These books are available anywhere books are sold online. Learn more on **www.PeggyMarceaux.com**

ERIN GO BRAGH
Publishing

Erin Go Bragh Publishing publishes various genres of books for numerous authors. Their portfolio consists of a 1200-page Vietnamese to English Dictionary, Historical fiction, an award-winning children's educational series, and an array of fun children's picture books, multiple adult novels and memoires, tween adventure stories, as well as Christian Fiction. Their objective is to promote literacy and education through reading and writing.

www.ErinGoBraghPublishing.com
Canyon Lake, Texas

www.ingramcontent.com/pod-product-compliance
Lightning Source LLC
Chambersburg PA
CBHW061251170626
46809CB00007B/2946